Heather Boyd

BESTSELLING AUTHOR

An Earl of her Own

Chapter One

Adam Croft scowled at the man striding along at his side through the church. "You're smirking."

"Am I, Lord Rafferty?" Gideon Whitfield asked, and then, still smirking, accepted the congratulations for his upcoming wedding to the Duke of Stapleton's youngest daughter. The announcement had delighted the congregation immensely, and the duke looked pleased as punch also. The ceremony would not be conducted in the village chapel but in the duke's nearby home.

"Definitely gloating," Adam noted as they moved on through the crowd. He nodded to the members of the congregation, those he recognized as locals. Adam attended Sunday services infrequently, but he'd had to come and see this. It wasn't every day that such a confirmed bachelor fell in love.

He nudged Whitfield in the ribs when the fellow continued to smile. "Anyone would think you are happy about today's announcement."

Whitfield laughed then. "Well, I am marrying the most remarkable creature in existence, so yes; I suppose I might just be a little happy."

Adam didn't bother to hide the fact that he rolled his eyes. "You keep saying that."

"You've only yourself to blame, too. Putting the idea into my head that I wasn't too old to make a match."

"The ideas were already in your head. You were just trying not to think about her that way," Adam gloated. Whitfield had been quite the idiot, and doing nothing to advance his cause regarding his admiration for Lady Jessica, but then again, all men were foolish when they fell in love. Adam had undoubtedly been the first time around.

They stepped outside into sunshine, and Whitfield sighed. "There's my angel. Would you excuse me, Lord Rafferty?"

Adam's eyes were drawn across the grassy lawn to where a group of ladies stood chatting together. Lady Jessica Westfall was a bubbly wench, and very popular. Her transparent happiness was almost embarrassing to watch as she welcomed her betrothed to her side. Lady Jessica acted as if they'd been parted for weeks rather than the passage of time required for a dull sermon and one short announcement.

The pair were obviously in love. Adam was pleased. He wouldn't wish a loveless marriage on anyone.

Adam turned away from the soon-to-be-married pair, and his eyes fell on the next lady in line behind them. Mrs. Rebecca Warner, the duke's daughter and a widow, was hovering around her younger sister, nothing unusual in that, but today there was a small, indulgent smile playing around her lips. Mrs. Warner rarely smiled upon anyone, and Adam actually thought she might approve of Whitfield for her sister.

Being somewhat taller than most—his mother had frequently referred to him as Mount Rafferty—Adam moved to stand slightly behind Mrs. Warner and out of the way. Mrs. Warner acknowledged him by the slight turn of her head in his direction.

He chose to speak first. "Well, Mrs. Warner?"

She turned a little more, and her smile vanished. "Well what, Lord Rafferty?"

Did he have to spell it out? Adam grinned. "What do you think about this pair making a match of it then?"

Her eyes drifted back to the happy couple, and her expression became one of intense satisfaction. "I couldn't imagine a better outcome."

Whitfield must have heard because he bowed to his future sister-in-law. "Thank you, Mrs. Warner," Whitfield murmured. "I'm still astonished by my good fortune."

"It was fate," Lady Jessica exclaimed, causing Whitfield's skin to redden with the beginnings of a blush. Lady Jessica smiled at Adam suddenly. "You will stay, won't you, my lord? Until the wedding? We want all our friends to be there for our happy day."

"I will be present for the wedding day, but I had intended to depart for home tomorrow," he told her. He had a daughter at home who was writing him letters, filled with recriminations for his absence and the occasional half-hearted threat to run away with the gypsies. His daughter had quite the imagination for only being ten years old, but her threats were empty ones. However, he wasn't about to test that theory. Her mother had been a rash creature in many respects.

Lady Jessica turned toward her intended. "Oh, he must stay! Shouldn't he, Giddy? Lord Rafferty can keep Father company now."

Adam glanced over the crowd and found the Duke of Stapleton easily enough. His grace had taken on a wife after Christmas and there was a babe in her belly already. And Mrs. Warner had come home earlier this year. She normally didn't return to the estate until June. His grace would hardly lack company when there were so many about. "Is Stapleton really in need of distraction?"

"He is." Whitfield broke free of his betrothed and came to stand beside him. "He is marrying off his last daughter, and I'm becoming afraid of what he has planned for the wedding breakfast," Whitfield confided in a whisper.

"You must expect speeches and flattery and an abundance of toasts to the happy couple," Adam teased.

"That's only the start, I'm afraid. Stapleton has it in his head to organize a house party. A large one. Everyone is coming, apparently."

"I see," Adam rubbed his jaw. By "everyone," Adam assumed that meant all the duke's children, grandchildren, cousins, aunts and such. Could be a rowdy crowd indeed. If there was a house party of such magnitude about to commence, Adam certainly wanted to remain for it. "If I remember correctly, there was a grand party for Fanny when she married, too."

Whitfield leaned closer. "I had wrongly assumed he'd gotten the urge for such elaborate celebrations out of his system when he didn't hold one for Mrs. Warner's wedding."

Adam had forgotten that, but he nodded toward Lady Jessica. "The youngest is his favorite."

Whitfield made a sound of discontent and Adam nearly laughed at the poor man's plight. Whitfield preferred the quiet but marrying into the Duke of Stapleton's family wasn't going to begin peacefully. Becoming surrounded by the duke's boisterous family, and exalted members of the ton, too, were bound to discompose Whitfield. He patted his friend on the shoulder solicitously. "You'll survive."

"A true friend would remain to support me," Gideon grumbled. "When you tie the knot again I will not forget your attitude today."

Adam laughed. He was widowed, left to raise a delightful daughter alone. However, Ava could not inherit his title or estate. Adam would have to marry for a second time and hope again for a son and heir to succeed him. "Weddings are a harrowing business. I'll see what I can do to stay."

Carriages began arriving in front of the churchyard, and Whitfield hurried to collect his future bride. The duke's carriage filled quickly, and when it drew away without Adam, he discovered he'd have to share the next carriage back to Stapleton Manor with only Mrs.

Warner's company. He winced. She was still talking with the older women and had not noticed the others had left without telling her.

He moved toward her to offer his arm. "Mrs. Warner. The last carriage is ready to take us back to the manor."

She nodded then bid farewell to Mrs. Hawthorne and her daughters before turning to him. "Thank you."

Mrs. Warner set her hand on his arm and Adam handed her into the carriage, and then joined her, sitting on the opposite bench.

The coachman shut the door and tucked away the step. "Looks like we have a lovely day for a carriage ride," he murmured.

"Those clouds suggest we are about to get rained upon," Rebecca Warner said as she adjusted her shawl about her shoulders. "As quick as you can, Mr. Porter," she called.

Mrs. Warner was something of a pessimist and had never warmed to him. She was always mentioning a lack of some sort—real and imagined. She hardly ever smiled. "Every day brings a challenge," Adam advised her. "I prefer to look on the bright side and hope for the best in everything."

Finally, her gaze lifted to his. "Indeed."

Mrs. Warner's features were regular, though pretty, and the way she stared at a man could be a little unnerving at times. She was the most reserved of all the duke's family and the most modest, favoring plain colors and high necklines that hid her charms. Adam found her strangely comforting to be around. He had always known what she thought of him. She was transparent in her dislike and disapproval of the things he said just to rile her up.

He removed his hat once the village was sufficiently behind them and ran a hand through his dark, wavy hair. The church had become stifling before the sermons were half over. He enjoyed the feel of the wind in his hair—more so when he saw her expression of disapproval. "So Whitfield and your sister? Did you sense it coming, too?"

Her lips pinched together a moment before she spoke, but her eyes were fixed on his hat, where'd he carelessly flicked it aside on the bench, and then his hair. "No. Did you?"

"I suspected a partiality on his side some time ago," he confessed, noting the speed of the carriage had increased to comply with Mrs. Warner's demand for a quick return to Stapleton. "I thought it all in vain until she returned from London unmarried."

Mrs. Warner's lips pouted for a moment. She set her hand to the side of the carriage to brace for the upcoming sharp turn at the bridge. "Yes, opinions change with new experiences."

"And absence makes the heart grow fonder." Adam set his feet farther apart on the floor. Tensing in preparation for the turn as well. "I expect—"

The next moment, Adam heard a loud crack and was thrown to the side as the carriage started to tip.

His companion shrieked, and he scrambled to latch onto Mrs. Warner's slender body as she seemed most in danger of falling out of the carriage. "I have you."

That side of the carriage dropped even more as the carriage creaked and groaned.

Dimly, Adam was aware of the coachmen swearing around them, and the horses becoming panicked. Adam quickly got his bearings. Clearly, the carriage could roll over if the horses could not drag them to safety. There was a steep downward slope toward the stream at this particular spot and gravity would pull them to their deaths if something weren't done soon.

He tightened his grip on Mrs. Warner and glanced over his shoulder. "What the devil?"

"We've lost a wheel, my lord. Are you harmed?"

"Only our pride, Mr. Porter," Mrs. Warner complained but surprisingly remained unresisting in his arms.

But if the carriage rolled over they'd be

crushed. "Get her out now!" Adam ordered.

The side door was flung open above them and men reached for Mrs. Warner's hands. Since the slope would be steep for a woman wearing long skirts to hinder her feet, Adam set his hands to Mrs. Warner's backside and shoved hard.

Fabric rent, but Mrs. Warner fairly flew up and over the side to safety, he hoped.

"Give us your hands, too, my lord," Porter cried, but then the carriage slipped a bit more. "We're losing it."

The carriage was too heavy at this angle, and it would only become more so. "To hell with it. Save the horses!" he shouted.

Adam grabbed the high edge of the carriage and threw himself out.

The carriage dropped away suddenly beneath him, and he was falling.

Adam landed face down on the slope and slid a few feet before he could stop. Below him, the sounds of wood splintering abruptly ceased. He didn't dare look. He scrambled up the slope to the top before letting out a shaky breath and looking around.

The horses were unhitched but still panicked, stamping around the grooms as they fought to calm them. All the grooms seemed accounted for.

Porter rushed to help him stand and brush

off his attire. "Are you all right, my lord?"

Adam nodded, looking for Rebecca Warner. She seemed unharmed on first glance. "Well, that was exciting."

Mrs. Warner's brow wrinkled as she pulled her patterned shawl tighter about her shoulders. "You saved me."

He nodded. "What else should I have done, Mrs. Warner?"

Her frown deepened even more. "Thank you."

He bowed gallantly but then regretted the gesture immediately as the world spun. "Bollocks."

The lady's eyes flared in shock. "Excuse me?"

"My pardon." Adam mastered himself and then limped toward the grooms to glance down at the wreck. The carriage had been quite destroyed by the fall, possibly beyond repair. "I hope his grace wasn't too fond of that particular carriage."

"Unfortunately he was, my lord," Porter murmured, cap in hand. Some of the debris became caught in the current and they watched it float away in silence.

The view from this height began to unnerve Adam, so he took a pace backward from the edge. He felt immediately better. "Are any of the horses injured?"

"No, my lord. They all seem to be in order. Just a bit excited still."

"Good. Send the men and horses back to the stables with the news. The duke will wish to know about this as soon as possible."

Porter frowned. "What of you and Mrs. Warner?"

"I'll walk back." He turned to Rebecca for her decision.

"I'll walk with him," she agreed very quickly.

Adam's head began to throb as Rebecca fell into step with him. They moved off the gravel drive to walk the most direct route through the lush gardens. A few yards from the road, Adam needed to wipe his brow.

He kept walking, grateful when they moved into the shade of tall elm trees but damned if he didn't feel himself. "I think we both deserve a drink after that. Damn it's hot today."

"No, it isn't," she noted with concern. She stepped in front of him and he had to stop or barrel into her. "Your face is damp."

"It is not damp, madam. I'm sweating like a damn hog in an oven," he grumbled.

Her previously concerned expression instantly became one of annoyance. "They mean the same thing. One is polite. One is not."

Adam shook his head at her criticism and regretted it immediately. He staggered to the nearest tree trunk until the sensation of unsteadiness stopped the garden from swaying before his eyes. "Bollocks."

"Perhaps you should rest here a moment."

"I'm not a child to be babied," he insisted but her idea *was* appealing. He wiped a hand over his face and put his back to the tree. "I heard fabric rip as you were pulled from the carriage. You are uninjured, aren't you?"

She set her hand to the shoulder seam of her gown protectively, and he noted her shawl was tightly drawn around her shoulders. "My gown suffered some damage that will be easy to repair. It could have been so much worse if you'd let me fall."

"We were lucky," he promised. Very lucky. If Mrs. Warner had demanded the carriage top be employed to protect them from the rain she'd foolishly worried about, neither one of them might have made it to safety. If they'd been traveling any faster…

Adam shuddered. His head throbbed, and he put his hand over the spot but it only made it worse. He jerked his hand back, staring at fingers that were now bloody. "Devil take it!"

Mrs. Warner rushed to remove her gloves and reached for Adam's head. "Let me see."

"You are too small to see the top of my head." Adam took stock of himself. He did not feel at all steady, so he slid down to a sitting position and stretched out his long legs.

She made a clucking sound of disapproval

and kneeled beside him to stare into his eyes. "You are hurt, worse than you want to say."

Her soft green eyes were filled with real concern, something he'd never expected to see on her face. "Well, that is disappointing."

"Disappointing?" Rebecca immediately began searching through his hair for the wound, and he chose to imagine it a sensual caress until she spoke again. "You have a gash to your head that has bled. Dear God, you could have died."

"Always looking on the bright side," he murmured, and then noticed how close the lady was to his body. He inhaled slowly, delighted in this unexpectedly rare treat. Mrs. Warner had never been the friendliest sort. "You smell nice."

"Really, Rafferty," she chided. She suddenly slipped her hand inside his coat, rummaged in his pockets and began to dab at his head with the handkerchief she found there. "This is hardly the time to worry about my perfume."

"As you say, I could have been killed. Seems like an appropriate time for noticing the little things in life that please me." He felt pain and hissed. Eager for a distraction, he dropped his gaze to her shoulder—now bare of the shawl, which had fallen away unnoticed by the lady. The respectable garment Rebecca had worn to church, so stylish and modest, was less so now thanks to the accident. The struggle out of the carriage seemed to have ripped the seam apart, and her pale skin looked very soft and inviting. He curled his fingers into the skirt of her gown and held it. "Lovely."

She drew back to peer into his eyes again, and then she glanced down at his fist. "What are you doing?"

What was he doing? Adam had no idea, but he wasn't of a mind to stop. "I can't walk back to the manor just yet," he admitted. "Talk to me."

"Just sit there quietly."

"Never been good at being quiet or still, you know." He let go of the gown and lifted one hand. He brushed his knuckles up the outside of her leg, past her hip and across to her belly. Yes she was proving a good distraction from his injury. "Or good."

Mrs. Warner dragged in a shocked breath. "Rafferty!"

He struggled to meet her eyes, more amused by her outrage than chastised, and tried to ignore a horrible sensation churning in his belly. He would not cast up his accounts in her presence. "I do adore tangling with feisty wenches. You're always so pretty and proper on the outside. But underneath…therein might lie all the wickedness a man could ever desire. Have you ever given in to temptation since you were widowed?"

Chapter Two

"No. Most assuredly not," Rebecca hissed, entirely shocked by the Earl of Rafferty's insinuation. "I would never."

"Pity," he murmured. "I think you and I could have a great deal of fun together."

"Well. I don't think—"

Rafferty groaned.

"What's wrong now?"

Lord Rafferty did not answer, and she really looked at his face then, overcome by fear. His normally expressive face grew slack of animation, and she quickly untied his cravat and set her fingers to his hot throat. He had hit the ground very hard. Rebecca found his pulse easily and counted the beats as her own heart steadied again.

His chest rose and fell with each breath, and that was somewhat reassuring. He had only fainted. "Typical of you to get the last word,"

Rebecca grumbled. She scowled at him. "Wake up, my lord."

When there was no response, Rebecca raised her hand and, wincing, delivered a light blow to his cheek.

The earl didn't move a muscle, so she tried to rouse him with another. The harder blow jolted his head and, perhaps enjoying it too much, she slapped him a third time.

When he continued to ignore her existence in favor of remaining insensible, Rebecca wriggled around to kneel more comfortably and inspected his wound further. She reasoned that if he were out cold, he wouldn't feel any pain from her probing.

The gash was troubling but thankfully bled very little. After cleaning out the dirt she could see in the wound, a few stitches would be needed to make him whole again. Lord Rafferty would have a sore head for a few days, but he wouldn't feel the pain for long given the way he usually drank.

She grabbed his chin gently and turned his face toward hers. "You should never have suggested walking home when you were injured," she grumbled. "Wake up, please."

It did not weaken a man to show they needed help now and then. It proved them as human as any woman. However, Rafferty had put her safety above his own, and she owed him a debt of gratitude she could never repay. Because of that, Rebecca felt obligated to worry about his health.

She released his face slowly, brushing his smooth-shaven cheek with a gentle caress. "Don't you dare die before I return. If you can't walk back under your own steam, I'll have to get help for you."

She climbed to her feet and looked around. She could go back to the gravel drive but no doubt the grooms would still be reporting the accident to those at the manor. There seemed to be no one about on this part of her father's estate right now, either. Annoyed that she'd most likely have a long walk, and would have to leave Rafferty alone, she turned back briefly. She would get the last word, whether he heard her or not.

"Lord Rafferty, I should like to inform you I do not appreciate your behavior toward me. You flirt, quite obviously jests at my expense and only uttered to humiliate me." She stood straighter. "Please cease smirking at me, too. We both know you could not mean a word of any of it. If I did ever want a lover—and I'm not saying I've ever considered such a thing— I'd be more discreet than you know how to be. I am not so lonely that I'd fall into just anyone's arms. After the humiliation Warner dealt me, carrying on with that servant, making me a laughingstock in my own home, and then dying, I trust no man besides those in my family, and perhaps Mr. Whitfield, since he will be family soon. We will always remain at odds, you and I."

She frowned at that uncomfortable truth. Rafferty was often at Stapleton Manor visiting her father, and now so would she be. Not that anyone realized her circumstances had changed yet.

She ran her gaze over Rafferty's long limbs and broad chest. His lungs continued to fill with reassuring regularity beneath a horrid silk waistcoat—one of many in his wardrobe, she assumed. "Also, I do not like your waistcoats. They are all hideous, like the one you wear today most assuredly is. Why you continue to dress like a preening peacock at your age is quite beyond my understanding. Do you not care that your reputation suffers for the garish nature of your clothing? I suppose you must not. If you had a wife, she would tell you that they hurt the eye."

Rebecca took a deep breath, and then pressed her lips shut. Perhaps that was more words than she'd intended to ever speak to Lord Rafferty, but she did feel better for saying things she would usually have kept to herself.

She made sure to cover her bared shoulder with her shawl, and then, on second thought, tied it diagonally across her body to preserve her modesty. "I'll bring help," she promised as she strode off.

After a brisk walk directly toward the manor through the avenue of tall trees, she saw her father racing toward her. She waved, and he altered course to intercept her. "What has become of Rafferty?"

"He's injured."

Father groaned. "What did you do to him?"

She looked at her father in astonishment. "I didn't hurt him. He must have struck his head when he threw himself out of the carriage."

Father's eyes grew round, and he grabbed her hands, turning them up for inspection. Rafferty's blood was on the tips of her fingers. "Dear God, are you bleeding?"

"No. It's Rafferty's." She nodded. "He has fainted, too. I suspect he was dizzy at the scene of the accident but refused to ask for the help he needed. He won't wake up for me."

"That's not good," the duke warned unnecessarily. "Where did you leave him?"

"Not far away," she promised, turning in that direction. "Rafferty is sitting beneath a tree at the end of the avenue."

They turned back but Father quickly outdistanced her and reached Rafferty first. He knelt down at Rafferty's side. Rebecca arrived as the duke raised his hand to crack his palm against Rafferty's cheek.

"I tried that," she muttered.

Father did it again anyway. "Wake up, man."

Rafferty straightened suddenly. "What was that for?"

"You fainted," she informed the earl.

"I certainly did not faint. I was merely resting my eyes."

"Oh, you did faint," Rebecca insisted.

"Now, now, Becca. This is no time to squabble." Father got a better hold on Rafferty's arm and tugged. "Up on your feet, my lord."

Rafferty stumbled up to his six feet and whatever inches tall he was and then lifted a hand to his head, his expression twisted in pain. "Damn, that stings now. It damn well does."

"Keeping silent might keep the pain at bay," Rebecca advised as she found the gloves she'd discarded earlier. Rafferty cursed far too much.

Rafferty snorted. "Of course you would recommend that."

The earl draped one arm about the duke's shoulders. They were almost of the same height and seemed to move easily together along the avenue.

When the manor came into view, Rebecca breathed a sigh of relief to be home again.

At the door, a footman drew close but his eyes were wide upon her. He enquired after her health and, once assured she'd suffered no harm, he produced a letter. "This came earlier today by special messenger."

Upon reading the sender's name, she was filled with apprehension. Rebecca pocketed the letter before her father noticed. "Thank you."

The footman lowered his gaze to the floor. "Shall I send your maid to attend you, madam?"

"Yes, please do. Also, can you deliver Lord Rafferty his usual requirement—white wine for this time of day?"

"Very good, madam." The fellow scurried away, glancing back over his shoulder once.

"Mrs. Warner!"

She looked up at the sound of the duke's call. He and Rafferty had paused halfway up the staircase and were both looking at her. Rafferty was grinning now.

"Yes?"

"Perhaps you should retire to your room to change. Immediately."

She glanced down—and saw her undergarments were on display. Her face heated and she quickly tugged up her gown and retied her shawl over herself. "I will."

Clutching the shoulder of her ruined gown, she hurried up the staircase until she reached the gentlemen. Rafferty was no longer grinning; he was sweating again, as if the effort of movement was more than he could bear.

Although she didn't want to care, she could not help but feel she should be worried about him. He had saved her.

Rebecca fell into step with them, saw Rafferty safely to his bedchamber, and then hurried to her own. Once there, she rang for a maid and moved to the mirror. "Oh!"

She put her hands to her head and groaned. Her gown looked like she'd been running wild for days, and her hair, her crowning glory, looked like a birds nest! She found what few pins remained and ran her fingers through her hair until stopped by knots. Crestfallen that she'd been seen looking less than her best beyond her bedchamber, she turned for the wash basin to cleanse her fingers of Rafferty's blood. Then she sat at her dressing table to await her maid's assistance.

It was a short wait. Nancy arrived very quickly but her eyes grew round in shock upon seeing her. "Oh, madam, I've just heard the terrible news! Are you hurt?"

Her wrist had seemed a little tender but she was sure the discomfort would pass by tomorrow. "I'm fine, but my hair and gown did not survive unscathed. Can you help me?"

"Happy to," Nancy assured her and began to work her magic.

She put Rebecca's long hair to rights again, coiling it into a loose chignon, and removed the damaged gown with assurances it would be repaired by nightfall. She helped Rebecca into a new day gown and fresh slippers.

Rebecca sent the maid away before she read her letter.

Thank heaven she had, for the contents were not pleasing.

Her friend, Mrs. Charlotte Benning, claimed to have exceedingly good news to share. The widow was to journey to Bath soon and was to stay for the month of August. Rebecca was invited to join her there if she were not otherwise engaged.

Rebecca folded the letter and tucked it away in a drawer to answer later.

Rebecca's last stay in Bath had been an awkward holiday she'd rather not repeat. Charlotte Benning had arrived unexpectedly at Rebecca's door and claimed her holiday lease had fallen though. At such short notice, with no other acceptable accommodation found, Charlotte had asked to stay with Rebecca. Rebecca had felt obligated to agree because of their years of friendship but soon came to regret it.

Charlotte had been an amusing companion in the beginning of her stay, but less so after a week. In Bath, there had arisen addition living expenses because of Charlotte—expenses far beyond Rebecca's expectations or budget at that time. Charlotte had been distressingly slow to offer to pay her way.

During the most recent season too, Charlotte had continued to presume on Rebecca's kindness and her pocket book.

Rebecca was widowed but not wealthy. Her jointure income only stretched so far. She had been very happy to use her family as an excuse to avoid the woman ever since.

Rebecca would write a reply tonight, thanking Charlotte for the invitation but explaining her intention to remain at Stapleton for the foreseeable future.

Besides, she was needed here until the new year began at least.

Rebecca left her room and headed down the hall, only to come to an abrupt halt at the vulgar profanities flaming the air.

Concerned, she rushed forward to see what was amiss. Servants were lingering outside Lord Rafferty's bedchamber—listening in and laughing amongst themselves.

Rebecca scowled at them as she marched to his door, and they wisely fled back to their duties.

"Please, my lord. Just hold still a moment," the Stapleton housekeeper was begging.

"A moment? It's already been three damn long moments," Rafferty complained, "and you say you are still not done sticking that needle into my skull."

"But—"

Rebecca stepped into the room, noting there was only Mrs. Brown present to tend to the earl's injury. She scowled at him. "Kindly mind your tongue, my lord. You are in the presence of respectable ladies."

His gaze raked over her boldly and angry color flooded his cheeks. "Where the hell have you been?"

She shook her head at his question and met the housekeeper's gaze. "I must apologize for Lord Rafferty, Mrs. Brown. He appears to have lost his manners in the accident."

The woman nodded, but Rebecca suspected Mrs. Brown was quite upset and trying not to show it. She drew closer to the housekeeper, keen to offer her support and protection. Mrs. Brown was an indispensable servant for Stapleton Manor, Rebecca had relied on her since she was a young girl, and she did not like that she might feel threatened by one angry earl—even if he was hurt. "How goes the work on him?"

"I am almost done, madam. One more stitch, I swear."

Rebecca turned toward Lord Rafferty and peered at the wound on the earl's head. In this light, after being cleaned and half stitched already, it hardly seemed very serious now.

Lord Rafferty was being difficult, but the wound really did need one more stitch. Her lips twitched as she caught the housekeeper's gaze. "Are you sure it shouldn't be two stitches?"

Rafferty began to sputter and protest.

The housekeeper's eyes widened in alarm at the prospect, but then Mrs. Brown glanced at the wound again. "Do you really think it needs two more?"

"No, one more bloody stitch will do and then get the hell out of my room," Rafferty ordered rudely.

Rebecca clucked her tongue. "She's only doing her job, my lord. I'm sure you want the wound to heal neatly. Why, it would be most embarrassing to have a puckering lump on your head."

Rafferty closed his eyes with a sigh. "Cruel woman."

Rebecca winked at the housekeeper and saw the woman relax at last. "You can begin again."

Rafferty's hand shot out and grabbed Rebecca's wrist. "You will stay."

Although she had no reason to remain except to protect the housekeeper from further verbal abuse, she indulged the earl. She patted his hand solicitously. "You've been such a brave earl."

The housekeeper nearly choked on a laugh, but then devoted herself to the last stitch the earl needed. Rafferty's hold on Rebecca's hand remained painfully tight through it all.

"Nicely done," Rebecca murmured when Brown had finished.

"Thank you, madam." The housekeeper backed away from the bed quickly. "In a few days, I'll look at the wound again and decide when to remove the stitches."

"Excellent. Thank you."

The housekeeper smiled quickly and departed, closing the door swiftly behind her.

Rafferty exhaled slowly, and his grip on Rebecca's wrist eased. "Does it really look all right?"

Rebecca rubbed her tingling wrist as she examined the stitches again, noting the earl's hair was matted with blood in places. His hair and brow should be cleaned up a little before anyone else saw him. She fetched a wet washcloth, and then picked up his comb. "There was no need to be so difficult. Mrs. Brown has tended a great many wounds, and this will heal nicely provided it does not become infected. No one is yet to die under her care, I assure you."

Rafferty squinted at her and then the comb. "What do you intend to do with that?"

"There's blood on your face and your hair." Rebecca smiled tightly and began dabbing at his bloody skin carefully, and then his hair. The spillage wasn't too widespread, so it was only a matter of moments before she was satisfied. Once the blood had been removed, Rebecca carefully combed his dark hair into pleasing waves.

He looked up when she had finished. "Would my dying bother you?"

"I've no idea. Why do you ask?"

He smiled softly. "In the avenue, after the accident, you said you didn't want me to die."

She gaped. "You fainted."

"No."

If Rafferty had heard her plea that he not die, then he had possibly heard it all—her rant about him and the disappointments of her life too.

He waggled his brows, which she took as confirmation.

Oh, he was devious! Face flaming, she clenched her jaw a moment before speaking with forced civility. "Why would you pretend to faint?"

"I closed my eyes because the world was spinning, and I kept them closed to fight off a wave of nausea. I was not in a fit state for conversation with a lady of your delicate sensibilities. To be honest, I was desperate to say what was really on my mind at the time."

"Do tell?"

He shrugged. "I should like to clear up a

misunderstanding between us. What you said about me, before your father arrived, is quite incorrect."

"You should never have heard anything of the sort," she complained. "If you were a gentleman, you would have made your consciousness known."

"If I had appeared awake, I doubt you would ever have been so forthright." He winked. "I do not pity you in the slightest. I merely like the challenge of getting under your skin. For the record, it's my opinion that any man who turns his back on his lawful wife is an idiot. If you were mine, you'd be in this bed with me already."

She opened her mouth, but no sound came out. Even in his sorry state, he thought only of pleasures of the flesh. "Unbelievable."

"I can see that my confession has unsettled you, but I will not apologize for being blunt. I may not have an opportunity to be so again, so please bear with me. We're lucky to be alive, and I don't intend to waste another moment worrying about offending your delicate sensibilities." He sat up slowly. "You are an attractive woman, and I think you actually do like me."

"I don't. I—" He started to rise, and she held him down. "Where are you going? Stay in that bed, my lord."

"Now if only you would say that to me when my health is improved." He pointed across the room as he subsided again. "I'd like some wine to dull the pain. Please."

Rebecca shook her head. Rafferty was pickled more often than not. A few drinks and he might forget all about her and this improper conversation. "I'll fetch you a glass."

"Thank you. I could kiss the person who sent that bottle up."

Rebecca choked. She may have sent the wine but she did not want to kiss him. Rafferty's overfondness for spirits was something Rebecca thoroughly disapproved of. However, today she was feeling slightly more sympathetic than usual. Receiving stitches was never pleasant.

She handed him a measure, and when he drank the lot, she fetched the bottle and refilled the glass for him. "Your valet should be summoned to look after you."

"I sent the fellow away. He's an expert at polishing my boots to a high shine and starching a neck cloth, but he's useless for ailments. Stomps his way through my chambers all the time, too. My head hurts too damn much to put up with that."

"Language, my lord." Rebecca sighed, realizing that for the moment, she was all the earl had. "What else can I fetch for you?"

"Now that you mention it…" Rafferty's eyes lit up with excitement—eagerness. When his outstretched hand brushed her hip, she dodged him easily.

"Not that," she chided, shaking her head in exasperation. "Can you only think of one thing?"

"Naturally, I'm a man." He chuckled softly and drank the remainder of his second glass. "It seems a little bright in here."

Rebecca went to the tall windows and drew the curtains closed, throwing the room into near darkness. Once her eyes had adjusted, she returned to the earl. "Anything else?"

"The bottle," he admitted quietly. "Bring it to me."

She picked up the bottle again, but Rafferty wouldn't let her refill the glass.

He sighed and held out his hand. "I appreciate your assistance more than words can say, but you don't need to see me at my worst. You should go. My head is killing me."

"Very well." She looked at the bottle and reluctantly handed it over. "Shall I have another sent up, too?"

He didn't drink from it immediately, but he didn't look at her again. "Probably should. Thank you."

She nodded, appreciating his restraint in her presence. "Do you need anyone to sit with you, keep you company?"

"No, thank you." Rafferty's gaze darted toward her, and a shy smile twisted his lips. "I will rely on my imagination and the memory of your tender concern to comfort me."

Rebecca threw up her hands. "Oh, you are impossible."

He quickly caught one and brought it to his lips. "Do you realize my late wife would have left me completely in the servants' care, were she still alive today?"

Rebecca blinked as Rafferty kissed the back of her hand. "Surely not," she gasped, breath coming fast.

Rafferty smiled slyly as he released her. "You wouldn't be the first to be surprised by that. I thought most wives the same until recently."

"I thought yours a love match," she admitted. "We all did."

"That is what my late wife wanted everyone to think," he confessed, looking away. "She loved the attention and envy of other women, so when she talked of our marriage, it was always with substantial embellishment of her part in it."

Lady Rafferty had seemed an ideal wife, and Rafferty a devoted husband. Apparently, Rebecca had been wrong. "You didn't love her."

"I adored her until the very end," he said, so quietly Rebecca shivered. He sounded so sad, and she was trying to think of a response when his gaze lifted. "Run along now and let me get drunk in privacy."

"Of course." She dropped a curtsy to Lord Rafferty. "My lord."

He leaned in her direction. "But do come back when I'm feeling better, and we can continue our discussion. Do you hate sleeping alone, too?"

"Yes," she said without thinking, and Rebecca's face flamed with embarrassment. That was too bold. She did not talk like that, or discuss the regrets she harbored with anyone.

She turned away for the door on legs suddenly no longer steady.

At the doorway, Rebecca glanced back once, only to find Rafferty watching her closely. She waved her fingers at him like some silly nitwit with a beau and then fled into the hall.

Once outside, and confident she was alone, she shook her head. Lord Rafferty was a worse flirt than she'd ever imagined; even injured, all he could talk about was pleasures of the flesh.

But what was genuinely unaccounted for was that she could still feel the touch of his lips on her skin even now.

Chapter Three

———— ♦ ————

Adam drank the afternoon away, acutely aware the pounding in his head accentuated a newfound dread for his own mortality. He might have died today. He would have died without an heir, too. Perhaps it was time to consider his future properly.

It was time to marry again.

Adam could not trust his future to fate. Even Whitfield knew he'd be the next man leg-shackled. Succession aside, there was also his daughter to consider. Adam couldn't leave Ava all alone in the world, at the mercy of a distant relations kindness when they inherit everything that should have gone to a son.

Adam leaned back and closed his eyes. He had hoped, no expected, to marry for love again. His first wife had appealed to him from the moment he'd laid eyes upon her sweet face.

He'd asked for her hand within weeks of that first meeting and had never regretted his impulsive decision.

He opened his eyes and looked about his empty room. If romantic love were denied him, Adam must choose with his head. But what qualities did he want in a second wife?

The answers came quickly. The lady he would marry had to have the right family connections, intelligence, obviously, a sweet, biddable temperament, and most of all they had to be compatible in the bedchamber. Someone nearer his age would be acceptable too. Giggling young ladies fresh on the marriage mart were a trial to talk to. He wouldn't want to bed one.

He also wanted someone who might come to care about him one day.

A lady he could tease.

He grinned suddenly, remembering the day in a completely different light.

Adam had flirted with Rebecca Warner today and survived to do it again. She had complained, of course, but still had shown real concern for his wellbeing. He had thoroughly enjoyed being the center of the woman's attention too, even if the peace between them couldn't last. Rebecca had made it plain on many occasions that she did not approve of him. As a wife Rebecca Warner would be unbearable. He'd never have a moment's peace.

Adam lifted his hand to his head and carefully felt through his hair for the wound. He must have hit his head harder than he suspected to be considering Rebecca as anything more than someone to annoy on occasion.

If he were truly foxed, out of his mind with drink, he would never consider the effort it would take to win Rebecca Warner's good opinion for any reason.

No, Rebecca Warner would never do for him as a wife. He probably shouldn't pursue her for a lover either. Rebecca was most definitely the marry first, kiss later sort of female. She would not fall easily into his arms.

He tossed the bottle aside in frustration.

No, Adam required wife not a lover. He needed a son to inherit Gable Park and his fortune. In a few short years, he would be launching Ava on the marriage mart also. He'd need help for that, so of course, a wife would help with the chore.

A knock sounded at the door, and he looked up slowly—almost excited that Mrs. Warner might have returned to check on him but discovered her father instead. He was profoundly disappointed by that.

The Duke of Stapleton waited at the open door, a ready smile on his face. "Can I come in?"

"Assuredly." Adam sat up straighter when he noticed the duke had a fresh bottle in his hand. "Is that rum, perchance?"

"Indeed," the duke murmured as he uncorked the bottle, and Adam caught the scent a moment later.

"Thank you." Adam needed a stronger beverage to get him through the long and lonely night ahead. He had been feeling sorry for himself since the accident. And since Adam's confession to Rebecca about his late wife's fickle nature, he had become unwisely nostalgic, too. He missed being married, even if his union hadn't been ideal in the end. He was glad of the distraction a new bottle brought, and his host, too. "The bottles of sweet wine you sent up earlier have done their job, and I'm ready to continue."

The duke frowned. "I didn't send any wine up to you."

"Ah, well, whoever it was knows my tastes well."

The duke smiled and handed over a refilled glass. "How are you feeling now?"

"I'll be right as rain soon enough."

"Good."

Adam sipped the stronger beverage slowly, relishing the taste. A few of these and thoughts of what he'd put himself through soon would indeed be banished from his mind tonight. The marriage mart was no picnic, and he'd be returning for the season to survey the available ladies every year until he had chosen a wife. Stapleton had had it blessedly easy. "So the announcement was made but have you really made peace with your youngest's decision?"

The duke scowled and strolled to the window and looked out. "She gave me little choice in the end."

"And Whitfield? Have you really forgiven him?"

The duke continued to stare out the window and didn't answer.

Adam swung his legs off the bed and stood slowly. He was very pleased the world was steady again because he'd had as much lying about as he could tolerate for one day.

He shuffled to the window to see what kept the duke's attention.

Out on the lawn, in full view of everyone at the manor, Whitfield and his future bride were holding what seemed to be an enthralling discussion as the sun set. Adam remembered those sweet moments fondly. Holding hands, stealing kisses, and the later discreet encounters that made falling in love so easy. For him, those heady days hadn't lasted much beyond the first year.

"No one can help who they fell in love with."

"It's an adjustment." The duke looked at Adam and nodded. "But there's no turning back now. Besides, what does it matter anyway whether I'm happy or not?"

Adam shrugged. "I wanted to make sure all is well before I ask for a favor."

The duke narrowed his eyes. "What sort of favor?"

"I've been away from home too long, and if I'm to stay until the wedding occurs, I'd like to send for my daughter to join me here."

The duke's brows rose high. "She's always welcome to visit when you come. I should have thought to say so before."

"Good. Ava's had little to do with society, and it is high time she met your grandchildren. The wedding seems an opportune time for them all to become acquainted with her."

The duke laughed softly. "And you miss her."

"Indeed. As much as you will miss your daughters when they all leave you."

"Well, there's to be another child by winter, so I imagine I'll never be alone again for the next twenty years." The duke grinned. "The more the merrier, I always say."

Pleased that Ava's arrival wouldn't be an imposition, he considered the upcoming house party. The Westfalls were a large family with many branches to be found in all corners of

England and Ireland. Adam hadn't met half of them yet, and he'd known the family at least twenty years or so now. "How many are coming to stay for the wedding?"

"A goodly number but none of the Irish lot, of course. They'd never arrive as fast as my daughter wishes to be married, but I'm sure they'll understand."

"But your heir is coming with his children?"

"Milo had better bring them this time. No doubt Samuel is coming with the twins, so unfortunately, Lady Ava will have the worst of my lot to contend with. I'm not sure about the other guests yet."

Lord Samuel's twins were said to be a handful, a pair of rebels in the making. "I'm sure she'll manage."

But Adam worried about his daughter a great deal anyway. She had no one but servants for guidance until he married again. His influence wasn't the same as having a mother to advise her how to be a proper lady.

"It's hard not to worry about your children, especially when they're stubborn," the duke admitted.

Adam considered that. "Ava isn't stubborn. Not yet, anyway."

"Give her time and appreciate these carefree days." His grace chuckled. "It's when she's out in society and later that you'll lose a great deal of sleep over her."

"Was Lady Jessica so worrying for you?"

"They all worry me."

Adam laughed softly and leaned a little to the side and hooked his finger into the collar of his discarded coat. "I suppose it is natural for fathers to worry, no matter their offspring's ages."

"What do you think you're doing?" the duke demanded suddenly.

"What does it look like? I'm dressing."

The duke took Adam's coat from his fingers. "You're not leaving this room."

"I am. I owe my daughter a letter, but I've nothing to write it with here. I am going to the library, and then I think I might find a comfortable chair to drink the night away."

The duke unexpectedly helped Adam put on his coat as if he were a valet. "I know just the right room for you. Quiet, out of the way. I'd be happy to join you later."

"Thank you, but that won't be necessary." It occurred to him suddenly that if he married again, his new wife might have been with him while he drank the pain away. Or maybe if he was married, he might not want to drink so much.

Adam collected the bottle of rum and tucked it under his arm. "Lead the way, your grace."

Halfway down the stairs, they met the duchess, who was on the way to her own rooms. It was clear as day that the duke and duchess liked each other. When the duke promised to follow her once Adam was settled, and then watched her walk away, Adam stifled a laugh.

"How did you do it? Forget that once upon a time you had a life with someone else."

The duke raised a brow. "A second marriage is not lesser than the first. It takes courage to consider such a change, but I really had nothing to lose. I fell in love again quite painlessly, I assure you."

Adam smiled at the way the duke described the upheaval of taking on a wife. The arguments, the compromises that must be made. Not all marriages were peacefully lived. "I always thought marriage was about finding someone you wanted to annoy for the rest of your life."

The duke roared with laughter and gestured to the back of the manor, instead of the library. "That's a unique way of putting it."

Adam rubbed his jaw. The duke had married his daughter's companion, Mrs. Gillian Thorpe, after more than half a year of knowing each other. Her grace had no fortune or exalted connections to speak of at the time. If she hadn't been employed here, the pair might never have met or married. There had to be a reason behind his sudden decision to remarry. "Proximity, I suppose, helped with your pursuit."

The duke smiled, a hint of roguish victory in his expression. "Of course. How else can a man in want of a wife capture her attention if he is never near her?"

The chase was often half the fun but the reward was always sweet. "I'll keep that in mind."

"It did help that we had something of mutual interest to talk about from the start."

"Such as?"

"My daughter."

Adam laughed softly. "I happen to have one of those. She could do with some mothering too, I suspect."

"I'll give you only one piece of advice about making a second marriage. Make sure your daughter likes the lady you mean to give your heart to. When they don't, it causes uncomfortable friction in the family."

He had suspected he might need Ava's approval, and it was a reason he was hesitant to begin a search. Finding a woman who pleased both him and his family was no small feat. A favorite aunt of his had refused to speak to him from the day of his first marriage until his late wife had been buried. In the duke's case, Adam had a fair idea where the friction in the family most likely stemmed from. "You're speaking of Mrs. Warner."

"Why do you say that?"

"It's hard to miss the way the pair never speak to each other. Definitely frosty when they are in the same room."

The duke scowled darkly. "Rebecca dislikes change."

Adam had actually understood Rebecca's reaction to the marriage because, at first, Adam had wondered at the wisdom of the duke's choice, too. However, having spent more time with the couple, Adam saw little wrong in the match now. The new duchess was more timid than the last but always extremely courteous to all. She very obviously loved her second husband—which really was all that should matter in the end. Keeping that love, having it outlast the first blissful year, was never easy though.

"She'll come around."

"Rebecca and Fanny didn't speak for two years when they married. I have little hope for a speedy acceptance in my case. Rebecca idolized her mother."

Adam raised a brow in surprise, but they were at a doorway to a small, cozy drawing room behind the main staircase, and he held his tongue. He moved inside, eager to write his letter summoning his only child to join him for the party to come.

"You should have everything you need in this room," the duke promised. "I'm sure my daughter will not mind sharing under the circumstances."

Adam froze, one hand inches away from the catch on the writing desk. "Which daughter am I sharing the room with?"

"This is the room Rebecca prefers to use, but I'm positive she's occupied elsewhere right now. She probably won't notice."

She probably would. Adam kept his suspicions to himself as he bid the duke goodbye.

Adam wrote a brief letter to his daughter and advised her to pack her best gowns for the house party. Once his message was drafted, he sealed the letter with the blue wax he found in the desk and waved it about until dry. As he waited, he noted a small collection of papers to one side of the writing desk.

Curious, he pulled one sheet toward him and found a list of expenses, meticulously kept in such spidery script that he had to squint to read. The pages reminded him of the shock of tallying his late wife's spending each quarter. He did not miss those arguments, or her attempts at evasion when he'd politely asked her not to bankrupt the estate for the sake of impressing her friends and family.

He put the sheet back as he found it and rose to his feet.

"I thought you were resting?" Rebecca asked suddenly.

He stilled and then turned around. "I still am. But I desired a change of scenery."

"The best views are out the windows." She looked behind him to the desk, one brow rising. "What are you doing there?"

"I needed to write a letter."

Her brow puckered. "Are you finished writing it?"

"Yes," he murmured, collecting his letter and waving it in the air to show her. "I just need to summon a servant to deliver it to Gable Park."

Rebecca nodded. "If you will excuse me, I need to retrieve something of mine from the desk, and then I'll be on my way again."

Adam quickly grabbed his bottle of rum and got out of the way.

As Rebecca bent over the desk, shuffling papers, his cock perked up when she seemed to waggle her derriere in his direction. She had not meant to do it, of course, but Adam couldn't seem to look away. Rebecca Warner was a nicely shaped wench, pleasant to hold. Her lustrous brown hair—quite long, he suspected—was elegantly coiled at the back of her head. She had a narrow waist, he knew, from the carriage accident, and an ample pair of breasts that he imagined would fill his hands nicely.

He looked up at the ceiling and cursed softly. "I must be mad," he muttered.

"What was that, my lord?"

"Oh, nothing." Adam stuck a finger into his collar to loosen his cravat. He turned away to look out the nearest window, too, in a bid to get his ardor to cool. "I was just thinking out loud."

"About the view?"

About *her*. Rebecca Warner drew his attention—and it wasn't just today, either. The haughtier she acted, the more appealing she seemed, and the more he wanted to annoy her, too. He feared he was becoming infatuated with the idea of bedding her. To do so would be a delicate undertaking. He'd never heard of another gentleman succeeding with her—or even trying, for that matter. He'd be the second brave soul perhaps to win the honor of bedding her, if successful. Maybe the luckiest man still alive? "The views at Stapleton are quite lovely."

"Indeed. Father is very proud of the gardens."

He turned slowly and set the bottle aside. He noted the lady's appeal was not diminished by her factual reply. She gave a man no encouragement whatsoever, and he didn't even mind. It was no wonder she had not remarried. She had an excellent pedigree and was hardly penniless—not that he knew her situation with any certainty. Still, a duke's daughter should have been sought after for a wife long before now.

Adam expected to be rebuffed should he attempt to seduce her, but the devil in him wouldn't quit whispering in his ear that persistence often won the day. Rebecca had been a widow some years now. He recalled hearing about her husband's infidelity, tupping a servant behind her back, causing an embarrassing scandal. Rebecca probably lived a moral life in response to that, and he suspected that might be why she remained a widow still.

Adam believed he would have no trouble pleasing her in bed should she extend him an invitation. But would she ever? Rebecca was undoubtedly a challenge—and he'd not had a worthy one in some time.

He held her stare until she seemed to squirm. "It is not just the gardens that I admire here."

Her lips parted slightly but then her brow puckered again. "Are you foxed?"

"Oh, absolutely," he promised without shame. "And I intend to stay that way for the rest of the night, madam."

"Typical of you." She glared at him, censure in her gaze, before looking back at her papers. She scooped them up with an unhappy grumble.

Adam did not mind when Rebecca pointed out his failings. He was often deep in his cups. The duke was an excellent host and encouraged his companions to indulge to excess. Or he had before his second marriage. Rebecca certainly had noticed his enthusiastic participation on past occasions and scowled constantly for it, too. To get closer to this lady, or any lady at all, he might need to curtail certain pleasures that he usually relied upon to cure his loneliness. A small sacrifice. What would it hurt to try to please her just once?

Since delicacy had never been his way, he chose not to mince words now about his intentions. "I tell you only so you might be forewarned not to expect too much from me right now. I would not perform at my best in such a state."

Her eyes narrowed. "What reason could I have to worry about your performance? You don't play an instrument."

"I could be tempted to play your body, if invited." He drew closer to her, enjoying the challenge she presented and her shocked expression.

Rebecca's eyes widened as he approached, but she didn't draw back or let him out of her sight for one moment. "You have mistaken me for someone else."

"Impossible, madam." He stopped inches away and inhaled deeply. The familiar scent of her perfume tickled his nose. She was refreshingly predictable. "You could invite me to your bed tomorrow night."

Her lips parted, but no sound came out.

Sensing a chance, he reached out one hand and brushed his fingers across her soft cheek. She seemed frozen in place. He'd expected only one reaction—for her to move out of range. Since she remained, Adam bent his head down a little more.

When she still did not move, he smiled. "I knew you liked me."

A delicate hand landed on his chest, and she shoved him back hard. "Eh, you stink of the bottle!"

He nodded but cursed the unfortunate timing of his decision to try to kiss her today. If not for the drink on his breath, he might have received that invitation. "I promise you, I won't next time."

Chapter Four

People in love could be so foolish, and the proof was practically dancing at Rebecca's side.

"Oh, Rebecca, you were so right that he would come around," Jessica gushed yet again.

"Indeed I was. Whitfield is perfect for you." Rebecca sighed deeply as they headed for the duchess' parlor. There was so much to do for the upcoming wedding, but her mind would not settle. She was still feeling a little shaken by the events of yesterday.

First, she'd almost been pitched out of a carriage. She could have died or been severely injured.

And second, possibly the most alarming development of her entire life, the Earl of Rafferty had tried to kiss her.

Rebecca was not the sort of woman who inspired scoundrels or whom seducers tried to charm on a regular basis. In fact, it was quite some time since she'd ever suspected a gentleman of her acquaintance considered her for such a dubious honor. That it was Lord Rafferty, a man Rebecca did not approve of, was even more perplexing—as was her reaction to him. She was ashamed to say that she was so stunned by his behavior, she'd taken too long rejecting his advances. Thankfully, the pungent aroma of spirits had enveloped her as he'd leaned down and delivered a reminder of exactly why she didn't trust him.

Men always did foolish things when they were deep in their cups, and hopefully he would remember none of it today to make their next meeting awkward.

Jessica rushed forward and spun in a circle. "Oh, I never imagined I could love anyone as much as I do my Gideon."

"So you said yesterday on the way to church, and this morning at breakfast, and now again here." Rebecca eyed her sister wearily as she caught up. She was starting to wonder if Jessica would talk of Mr. Whitfield's perfect nature from morning till night for the rest of her life. "Perhaps a little less gushing might be appropriate."

Jessica clutched her arm and laughed at her rebuke. "Am I unbearable?"

"Only a little." Rebecca had always been amazed by how easy Jessica's life was. Bad luck seemed to follow Rebecca lately like a plague. But everyone worried that Jessica was happy, and it was nearly impossible to hold a grudge against her. "I'll forgive you if you tell me that you've finally settled on the exact date you'll marry."

"Yes, we've decided on May sixth. Father believes we will have a special license by then. If we allow a few days for delays because of any poor weather, the date seems the most reasonable."

And blessedly soon, too. Rebecca made a quick calculation in her head of the distances their siblings must travel and nodded. There would be just enough time for only immediate family to attend. "I have already prepared an initial itinerary for the day."

"Did you show Mother?"

"The duchess was with me when I drafted the initial plan. She still has it."

Jessica glanced at her sideways. "You and Mama are getting along better now."

"I suppose we are." Rebecca sighed though. There was no escaping the fact that their usually sensible father had married a common-born servant he'd recently employed. There was nothing to be done about it now. There was a babe in the duchess' belly. Rebecca had to accept the change for the sake of the child and the family.

Rebecca might not entirely approve of the new Duchess of Stapleton yet, but so far the woman had caused no embarrassment or scandal for the family, which had been her initial fear. Her grace did seem open to suggestions on how things must be done, which was a relief. Rebecca had expected a battle over a dozen little things but so far so good.

Jessica tapped on the door to the duchess' parlor and waited for an answer before pushing the doors open wide.

Rebecca gaped in surprise at what they found and quickly looked away. Jessica, however, just sailed inside.

Rebecca risked another peek. Her father was on the settee, and the duchess was draped against him. They looked cozy. Intimate. The duke should have told them both to come back at a later time.

"I thought I should have to send another pair of servants to find you," Father complained

"We were out taking a walk together," Jessica hastened to say as she flopped into a chair near their father.

Rebecca hesitated and remained on her feet. "If we are disturbing you now, we can come back at a later time."

"No, no. Now will do nicely." Her father gestured to a chair, and Rebecca sat in it quickly.

The duchess squinted at her. "Are you sure you were unhurt in the accident?"

"Yes."

"Then what is wrong with your wrist? You've been favoring it ever since the accident."

Rebecca looked down at her hands and saw the way she was holding herself. It seemed the duchess was more observant than Rebecca's own family. "It's nothing to make a fuss over."

Her father stood quickly and held out his hand to her. "Let me look at you, Rebecca."

Ignoring her father's request was impossible so she put her hand in his.

Rebecca had not wanted to talk about the accident or those few moments where she had been in danger of losing her life. If she had fallen, the carriage would have crushed her, and the earl, too.

Father gently manipulated her wrist, and she winced when he bent it in such a way that caused pain.

"It is only strained, your grace. Lord Rafferty grabbed me to pull me back to safety, as did the grooms helping me out of the carriage. I'm sure by tomorrow, any discomfort will be gone."

Father's eyes widened. "You should have had the housekeeper look at it."

"I'm quite capable of looking after myself. Besides, Lord Rafferty's injury was much more severe and he deserved all the attention." She pursed her lips. The man had saved her life then tried to seduce her while drunk. Good manners dictated she at least ask after him once. At the most. "How is Rafferty today?"

"Fine. Fine. Rafferty has suffered no lasting harm." Father shrugged. "He ate a hearty breakfast with me earlier and has gone off to call on Whitfield."

"You should have told us you were hurt," Jessica grumbled. "I could have been of use to you last night, and instead you let me prattle on about Gideon."

Being fussed over was never pleasant. That was why Rebecca had not mentioned her injury. She'd learned her lesson well in childhood. When Rebecca was younger, Father had her confined to bed for far less. "I promise you, I am well enough," she murmured before looking at her father. "You wanted to hear about the plans for the wedding."

"Indeed." He reached for a folded sheet of paper and handed it over. "And I've written down some early thoughts for the celebrations."

Rebecca studied her father's scrawling penmanship, and her eyes widened at his unexpected requests. She sank back into her chair. She gulped at the nonsense written down. "You want all of this arranged by the sixth?"

"We can put off the wedding a bit." He pointed to the page. "There's more overleaf."

Rebecca flipped over the page and saw a long list of names. "You want to invite all these people, too?"

"Yes."

Rebecca wet her lips and exchanged a long glance with her sister. The future bride seemed disappointed—by the delay, she thought, rather than the guest list. As a bride, surely Jessica was more interested in claiming the groom than a grand party. "Excuse me, Father, but this is…too much."

"You feel I should do less for your sister?"

Indeed she did. Father had a tendency toward extravagance where his amusements were concerned. The cost of this wedding would bankrupt a less-wealthy family. Rebecca hadn't allowed such an unnecessary fuss to be made when she'd tied the knot. "In the time we have before the date Jessica and Gideon hope to be married, it would be impossible to arrange even half as much."

Her father snatched the list back and looked down at his notes. A frown line instantly appeared between his brows. "What would you suggest be cut?"

Three-quarters of the list, for a start. Rebecca considered what might be the most obviously wasteful expense. "Well, I don't believe there needs to be two orchestras playing on the wedding day."

"I thought we'd host a ball and have two playing at once—one outside on the lawn, the other inside as usual. That would be very pleasant for the revelers."

"May I see the list, Nicolas," the duchess asked suddenly in a firm voice.

The duke obediently handed it over and then sank down beside his wife.

Rebecca held her breath as the new duchess read her husband's wishes. The woman's eyes slowly widened. Was this the first time she'd heard of this nonsense, too?

The duchess straightened after turning over the page. "Really, darling. Mrs. Warner is correct. It would take half a year to arrange most of this properly. I doubt Jessica would be happy to wait so long for her happy day. The sixth is a perfectly reasonable length of time to wait to be married by special license."

Was her grace going to be Rebecca's unexpected ally in this?

"But—"

The duchess placed a restraining hand on her husband's thigh. "Leave it with me. I am certain your daughter and I can figure out a way to celebrate Jessica and Gideon's wedding day without bankrupting the family."

The duke frowned again. "I wanted to stay and help."

Her grace smiled in response. "And you have. Completing arrangements for a house party should be my responsibility."

"Yes, but this is a wedding. You've not been

well, and I thought—"

"I am better now, and it's time I started doing my duty."

"You know I don't care—"

The duchess placed a finger over the duke's lips. "I will do this."

"Well, all right. If you're sure you don't need me."

"Not for this," she murmured, brandishing the sheet. "We'll organize the most beautiful wedding possible for Jessica. I promise. Off you go. I'm sure you have more pressing matters on the estate than fussing over me."

"I married you so I could take care of you," he promised before kissing her brow. The duke stood and drew in a breath. "I did promise to meet the stable master soon."

"You shouldn't keep him waiting."

Father kissed his new wife goodbye and then strode off.

The duchess lowered her eyes to read the list again. "A driveway lined with lambs wearing cravats? Never would I allow that."

"I had one as a pet," Jessica confessed to the duchess. "I used to dress it up and take it for walks."

"Like a dog," Rebecca muttered softly.

"Crystal jugglers, gypsies to bless the marriage?" The duchess covered her lips, but it didn't diminish the sound of her laugh. "Oh my. Well, there's no way we can allow those, either."

"But—"

"No, Jessica," her grace said, tone slightly harder than she usually used. "If you want pet lambs at your wedding, you will have to appeal to your betrothed to fetch and clothe them. Gideon is tolerant, but I highly doubt he will indulge you in that, either."

"It was funny," Jessica protested.

"When you were a child perhaps, but not now." The duchess smiled at Rebecca and handed the list to her. "Some of my husband's ideas are possible, but let us not turn a wedding into a country fair. Remove the most costly and bizarre of his suggestions but ensure the wedding date is set for the sixth."

Rebecca moved to a writing table and transferred Father's most sedate requests to her own list. "Manageable. But only barely. There would never have been enough room at the manor for all the guests father had initially wanted to invite, either."

"He's not always as practical as we might hope," the duchess lamented.

Rebecca agreed. The wedding would keep her completely occupied for over a week. Still, she rubbed her brow in anticipation of a headache to come from all this.

"I'm so sorry but I really do need your help

with this," the duchess murmured at her side.

"I would be happy to take it on for you." She looked up at the duchess. "We're going to need a private space to organize this wedding from. Might I move everything to the parlor I use for the next week or so? We can meet there each day to discuss progress and make decisions."

"Anything you need is yours." Her grace grimaced. "I'm also sure we don't need to invite your father along at first if you'd prefer he not be included in our discussions. Nicolas can be a little excessive."

"I have a lifetime of familiarity with my father's excesses," she advised.

"Good," the duchess returned to her chair and then suddenly moaned. "If you don't mind, Mrs. Warner, Jessica, I need to be alone for a little while."

"Are you unwell again?" Jessica asked.

Rebecca jumped to her feet and hurried her sister out the door. "Talking about being unwell inevitably brings that very result to pass," she reminded her sister. "Could you find the address for your seamstress and bring it to me? We'll need to write to her about your trousseau."

Rebecca shut the door just as the duchess suddenly acquired a basin that had been secreted beneath the settee and cast up her accounts into it. Rebecca rang the bell for a servant and then moved to open a window for fresher air. When she turned back, the duchess had sprawled back into a chair, panting. Rebecca fetched a glass of water and set it down beside her.

"Don't tell him," the duchess begged as she mopped her own brow. "He'll only make a bigger fuss and try to talk me back into bed."

Rebecca was surprised by her request but readily agreed to keep the secret. If the duchess did not want her husband around, who was Rebecca to argue? "He always fusses."

The housekeeper herself came to answer the summons in a rush.

While Mrs. Brown looked after the duchess, Rebecca observed the woman her father had married. She'd lost weight since they'd first met, on account of the babe most likely. Although the duchess' health was none of her business, she made a request to the housekeeper before she left the room. "Would you have Cook bake flatbread with a little honey mixed in for the duchess to nibble on?"

"Of course," the housekeeper nodded enthusiastically and rushed away to do her bidding.

"My sister-in-law swears by it," she explained to the duchess.

"Thank you. I'm willing to try anything to make this sickness stop."

"Oh, it won't stop you casting up your

accounts, but it will feed you up a little more."

"I was so hoping for a cure," the duchess admitted with a weary laugh. "I should know this, but should we add your husband's family to the wedding guest list?"

Rebecca shook her head quickly. They were not fond of her. They had taken Warner's side when his affair with their housekeeper had become known. They had blamed Rebecca for his actions, accusing her of abandoning her marriage and her husband. Of driving him into the only arms that welcomed him. They were quite ridiculous because that was not correct. "We are not on the best terms."

"I can sympathize." The duchess sighed. "When it became known that I had married so well, I received a begging letter from my late husband's family."

Rebecca was not surprised. "Did you give them very much?"

"I gave them what they gave *me* when Thorpe died. Five shillings, and then I reminded them of their request that I never contact them again."

Despite her reluctance to like the duchess, Rebecca wholeheartedly approved. Perhaps they were not so dissimilar after all. "A good response."

She turned away and spread the papers out on the table.

"What can I do to help you there?"

"For now, nothing, your grace. But later there will be much to talk about and for you to approve. Rest now," Rebecca suggested gently. She may never love the duchess as her sisters did, but she did not wish great ill upon her. "Sleep if you can while father is gone. Only time will stop the babe affecting you."

"I'll try, but it is so difficult to be idle. I've never been very good at doing nothing."

"I am the same."

The duchess fell silent. After ten minutes, Rebecca turned in her chair to look at the woman her father now loved. The duchess had fallen fast asleep, her arms curled around a small pillow, but the rounded curve of her belly where the child lay was clear. In sleep, Gillian Westfall seemed…not quite the villain Rebecca had once thought she might turn out to be.

She would make an adequate duchess if she continued to speak out against the duke's excessive spending, too. Father was generous to those he loved, but so far it seemed the duchess was sensible and could stop him.

Rebecca studied the list her father had given her, appalled by the extravagance he'd initially wanted. Did he not think of the future? It was his responsibility to pass the estate to his heir in the best possible condition.

And what of this next child to come? If a son was born, an education, the trappings of a gentleman and a healthy allowance must be given. If there were another daughter, the girl would require a dowry. Father had always been too generous to his offspring, in her opinion. A large enough dowry meant an advantageous marriage was a certainty, but it did not guarantee happiness.

She pressed her lips together as unexpected anger coursed through her.

Happiness was always short-lived and never should be taken for granted.

But a tear still slipped down Rebecca's cheek that happiness had eluded her.

She wiped it away as she glanced at the new Duchess of Stapleton's expanding belly. Now was not the time to dwell on what couldn't be changed. Her grace was lucky to have found a new life filled with love. Rebecca was not likely to ever be so lucky.

She only attracted drunken sots.

Chapter Five

One of Adam's favorite pastimes in London was patronizing the craftsmen who hawked their wares to an exclusive clientele. His favorite tailor was on Old Bond Street and was much sought after by those in society. Weston's was a fashionable place to spend a few hours, and he met friends there, too, sometimes. Here in the country, a gentleman must rely upon the local merchants to keep up appearances. But at least here, tailors would call upon a gentleman in his home.

Adam turned his head and smiled at the look of confusion on his partially clad friend's face. Whitfield was being fitted for a new suit of clothes today and did not seem particularly enthralled by the experience. Since his friend was about to be married, Adam expected to see that expression often. "You said she liked you in blue," Adam reminded him.

"Yes, but which blue?" Whitfield muttered in a bewildered tone, looking at the fabric samples spread about.

The tailor held up two blue swatches in slightly different shades. "Which of these do you prefer, sir?"

Whitfield squinted at the nearly identical colors.

Adam chuckled. "If you cannot choose between them, why not have both made up? A man cannot have too many waistcoats."

"Yes, we'll do that. One of each color, Mr. Hutchinson." Whitfield let out a pent-up breath and caught Adam's eye. "How's the head today?"

"Perfect," Adam promised. He still had his stitches but his head no longer hurt. He waved away the offer of wine when Whitfield pointed to a bottle and pair of glasses set to one side. "No, thank you."

Whitfield reapplied himself to holding still while the tailor pinned his chest with blue fabrics.

Adam had set himself the challenge of not drinking spirits until the dinner hour and limiting himself to drink only with the meal. Adam would not deny himself the pleasure of kissing Rebecca at least once in his life, and since she did not approve of his drinking, particularly the scent, he'd give it up for the next few days.

Adam replaced Whitfield at the mirror and considered his own appearance. Today's waistcoat was one of his favorites…light blue silk shot through with dark purple stripes. Adam thought he looked very well in it, but as he fiddled with the fit, he remembered that Rebecca would not agree. She'd called him a preening peacock after the accident. Not that he cared about her criticism exactly, but as he turned away from his reflection to study the fabrics strewn over Whitfield's bed, he decided another change might increase his appeal to her.

He addressed the tailor. "I have a commission for you, too, sir when you are done with outfitting Whitfield."

The tailor's eyes lit up with delight at the news. "If I'd known, I would have brought a different range of fabrics, my lord. The most daring were left behind at my workshop."

Adam studied the plain and sensible fabrics before him, colors that Whitfield usually sported, and took a deep breath before speaking. "Something from what you have will do. I need a few waistcoats made in a hurry. A dove gray, eggshell blue, and the pale yellow."

Whitfield chuckled. "What, no stripes or prints?"

Unfortunately not, if he wanted to impress the easily displeased Rebecca Warner. "No."

"What of the buttons? I have some elegant

gold and pearl buttons in my shop. I should have thought to bring them with me."

Ordinarily, Adam would choose either in an instant, but he shook his head. "Covered buttons."

"Covered with what, my lord?"

"The waistcoat fabric." He pointed at his friend's current attire. "Do them the way you do Whitfield's."

"But—" The tailor began to protest, but Adam shook his head.

"I refuse to outshine the groom on his wedding day."

Whitfield laughed and slapped his shoulder. "That will never happen, my lord."

Adam allowed Whitfield to harbor his delusions as their respective orders were made final.

When the tailor was on his way back to his workshop, Whitfield turned to him. "Are you sure you are all right?"

"Indeed I am. Now, how are you bearing up? Nervous."

Whitfield threw a scowl at him. "Not even a little."

"Good. I'd hate to have to drag you to the altar kicking and screaming that you're too young for marriage."

Whitfield shook his head. "No chance of that, but I *am* looking forward to the fuss being over."

"Marriage means a lot to women," Adam murmured. "The ceremony, the toasts, the wedding night and after. It all sticks in their heads. Beware, sir, they dwell on it later and use it against us, too."

Whitfield chuckled. "Are you suggesting men don't do the same thing?"

Adam remembered his marriage vividly—the good times and the bad. The pleasures, and the pain of loss. The negative aspects of marriage had always had him facing the other way. Whitfield had no idea what was in store for him, really. Marriage was an adjustment in so many ways.

"Perhaps we do, too."

Whitfield headed for the doorway. "I'm expected back at Stapleton."

"You certainly are, but I'll tag along." He grabbed his hat and gloves and hurried after his friend.

They headed outside into a garden lit by sunshine and stirred by a light wind. Adam glanced at the sky. Not a single cloud to mar the view. Mrs. Warner would be so disappointed. He smiled slightly. "How long do you think Mrs. Warner will remain at the manor after the wedding?"

"She's not said. Why do you want to know?"

Why indeed? "Just an idle question."

"However long she stays, I'm just thankful she approves of me marrying Jessica."

"Well, *I'm* glad she came alone this year,"

Adam murmured. "Those women she calls friends chatter so much they make my head hurt."

Whitfield walked along a few steps in silence before he spoke again. "I shouldn't mention it, I don't like to gossip about the family, but I think there must have been a parting of the ways a few months ago."

"Nothing serious, I trust."

"I'm not sure. Rebecca hasn't mentioned any of her usual companions when I've been around, and Jessica says she has no plans to see them anytime soon. That is unusual."

"How so?"

"Because in past years, she's taken great delight in telling everyone her travel plans," Whitfield noted.

"Rebecca does enjoy the social round. Many widows do."

Whitfield shrugged. "Jessica used to comment upon her going and often counted the days until she left again."

Adam winced. "I thought they were close."

"Close enough. Sisters don't always agree with each other, do they? Rebecca was a bit relentless about Jessica's preparation for her season, always mentioning how she had to make the right choice in a husband."

Adam smirked. "She chose you instead?"

"Surprisingly, Rebecca does not seem to mind that I'm not titled or terribly rich."

"Was a title really so important? Rebecca married a man without one."

"It seemed to be once," Whitfield shrugged.

At least Adam would have an advantage being titled and wealthy enough to choose any bride he liked. He wouldn't have the worry that he might not be an acceptable suitor if he made those few changes Rebecca had already warned him about.

They had reached the manor by then and stepped inside the cooler interior together. Adam turned for the room he'd occupied last night. He'd left his book there by mistake and was keen to recover it. He'd find a servant to return it to his room when he went in to luncheon later.

Instead of an empty room, Adam discovered Rebecca hunched over her writing table, dozens of papers scattered about her in a circle. She seemed not to notice his arrival, so he cleared his throat.

"Don't you have somewhere else to be, my lord?" she complained.

"Not particularly." He drew closer. "It's nearly time for luncheon."

"I am well aware of the time."

Since she did not lift her head, more interested in her writing than in conversing with him, Adam had time to study the woman. Her fingers were stained with ink, and a long lock of her hair had fallen, only to be tucked behind her ear. "What are you doing?"

"Considering the seating plan for my sister's wedding breakfast one more time."

He glanced over her shoulder—and his eyes widened. "That's a lot of people to accommodate."

"Less than it could have been," she muttered softly. "My father had a great many friends he wanted to invite at first."

He leaned a little closer and studied the arrangements she was making. Seating guests and organizing parties were matters best handled by wives. However, he didn't think he'd ever viewed such detailed notes before. He was impressed by Rebecca's meticulous attention to detail.

There was a page of notes for every servant. A timetable for the bride and family. Nothing was to be left to chance, it seemed. When he spotted his own name on a page assigned to a particular servant, he pulled the sheet toward him. On it, Rebecca had made a note regarding his preferences for certain types of drink at different hours of the day.

He hadn't known he was so predictable. It was accurate—or had been until today. "You are organizing absolutely everyone."

She tensed.

"I am in awe of your forethought," he promised.

"Really?"

Since that single word was drenched in sarcastic

tones, he hastened to explain. "Indeed. There is nothing worse than suffering the company of someone you routinely disagree with."

"I don't want to sit by you, either."

Adam laughed but pointed to a different name on her chart. He leaned close to whisper in her ear, "Lord Farrington bores me to death, and you've put him way over there. I cannot thank you enough!"

"You're welcome."

"You truly are a gifted hostess." He drew back and set his hands on the chair back. "Ever considered managing your own family?"

"I am."

He chuckled. The woman was impossible. "I meant have you considered taking on a new household. A husband."

Her head lifted, chin jutting out. "No."

"Shame," he murmured. He was disappointed. "I'm sure a man could grow accustomed to the idea of being managed so well if there were other compensations to be had."

Her brow furrowed, even if she kept her eyes on her papers. "I've no idea what you're talking about."

Adam pursed his lips, and then leaned closer again. "Sex, Becca. Hot, sweaty sex that lasts till dawn. Surely you remember how good it felt?"

Her lips parted, and she bounced to her feet. They were eye to eye then, but Rebecca was stuck between him and the table. She seemed at a loss for words.

Or had she no idea that sex could be so good? She had married an older fellow, a man well past his prime, after all, so perhaps she didn't.

"You should not speak to me like that," she finally said, cheeks turning a fiery red. Excitement or anger, Adam couldn't tell yet.

"What can I say, you bring out the devil in me. Figuring out what you want, what you desire, is going to be a challenge." He grinned.

"I desire you to find another to torment."

"But I like you," Adam confessed, and saw her eyes go wide with shock at his words. It was true. She fascinated him. "Invite me to your bedchamber tonight and find out if I can meet your high standards under the covers."

Her lips compressed into a tight line briefly and then she scowled. "I would never invite a scoundrel into my bedchamber."

Scowls could be attractive on the right face Adam discovered then. Rebecca Warner was no shy, biddable widow, eager to impress him—a wealthy earl. She had this fierce inner fire that rarely saw the light of day but when it did he was enthralled by her vibrancy. When she spun around, he leaned close to whisper, "Who needs a bedchamber? Any wall will do when the impulse strikes. One night soon, you should give me a chance to make you happy. After ten any evening would suit me very well. I'll be waiting with breathless anticipation for your signal. In the meantime, I'll keep you company."

The duke had said proximity was important.

Adam collected his book, settled into the same chair he'd occupied last night, and began to read. If not Rebecca, then some other lady would warm to him eventually. For now, he would practice on the most appealing lady to hand.

While he read, he could swear Mrs. Warner continued to glare at him for several minutes.

He refused to look up. He'd thrown down the gauntlet. In precise terms, so she had no doubts about what he initially hoped for.

He was still waiting for an invite half an hour later, when there was a knock on the door.

"Yes, what is it, Mr. Brown?" Mrs. Warner asked before he could.

"A special delivery for Lord Rafferty, madam."

Adam came to his feet. "Send her in, Brown."

"Her?" Mrs. Warner queried.

He tossed his book aside. "My daughter."

The light of Adam's life, Ava, rushed into the room. He grunted at the impact of her small body against his but tossed her up into his arms easily enough. "You got my message?"

"I did." The girl kissed his cheek loudly and

wrapped her arms tightly about his neck. "I thought you were coming home yesterday."

"I had a tiny mishap," he told her, patting her back. "Nothing to worry about."

She drew back, frowning. Ava had his eyes but her mother's slighter build, thank heavens. Today, her long hair had been pulled back—but then he noticed what she was wearing, and scowled. "What did I say about wearing those breeches beyond the estate? They are only for fencing lessons."

"I'm sorry, Papa. Don't be cross." She looked so honestly distraught he held his tongue to hear her excuse first. "I had to take my lessons before I left but then the carriage was ready and my luggage loaded. I was already in the carriage before I realized I'd forgotten to change."

His daughter could be flighty at times, a whirlwind of excitement. He would have preferred she not look like a hoyden, but there was no pretending she wasn't occasionally.

He reluctantly glanced beyond Ava, expecting to see disapproval. Rebecca and the butler were watching them. The butler was trying not to grin. Rebecca's expression had become utterly unreadable though.

He eased his daughter down to her feet and turned her about to face the sort of woman Ava might have to impress one day, bracing for the worst possible introduction ever. "Mrs. Warner, I don't believe you have met my daughter, Lady Ava Croft of Gable Park. Ava, may I introduce Mrs. Rebecca Warner, one of the Duke of Stapleton's daughters."

"Oh," Ava squeaked as she stepped out of his reach.

Rebecca drew closer, eyes skimming over his girl from head to toe—but then a sudden smile burst over her face as she curtsied. "A pleasure, my lady."

"A pleasure indeed, madam," Ava replied before dipping into a curtsy that wobbled just a little.

Rebecca's smile diminished very slowly. "I trust you enjoyed your lesson, my lady?"

"Oh, I did!" Ava told her with unabashed excitement.

"Do you practice the sport often?"

Puzzled by Rebecca's mild tone, Adam raised his eyes quickly. She seemed not to disapprove—at least not yet.

Ava nodded enthusiastically to the other woman. "Yes, madam. Every day. It's invigorating exercise."

Rebecca's brows lifted a little. "Indeed it is. Have you ever fenced against a real opponent?"

"Only Papa, and only once because I cut him."

"A shallow cut," Adam hastened to add. Ava had been upset enough over the incident.

Rebecca clucked her tongue. "You should know better than to fence with real weapons without adequate protection, my lord."

"I know that now. At the time, I hadn't realized how quickly my girl could swing the blade. A mistake I have not made again."

Ava's face fell. "I may only use wooden swords now."

"It is not the same, is it?"

Ava shook her head solemnly. "It is not the same at all, madam."

A soft laugh escaped Rebecca's lips suddenly. "Mistakes teach us to use better judgment."

Adam cleared his throat. "His grace allowed me to send for my daughter. She's going to stay for the wedding."

"I do wish he'd informed me earlier. Excuse me." Mrs. Warner turned away to sit at her table again before Adam could decide if she was annoyed or not that his daughter was a late addition to the party. She pulled several sheets of paper toward her and studied them carefully.

Ava edged nearer to him, slipping her hand into his larger one. "Is something the matter, Papa?"

"Nothing is wrong, my dear," Mrs. Warner answered for Adam. "I just need to decide where best to place you in the house. With all the guests coming for the wedding, it's a little complicated."

"She could have my chambers."

"That will not be necessary, my lord. Besides, I would then have to find somewhere else to put *you*." Rebecca made some notes on a page. "There. Brown, will you place Lady Ava in the Primrose bedchamber? The room next to mine."

Adam stepped forward. If his daughter slept in the chamber next to Rebecca Warner's, any seduction attempt would fail before it could truly begin. "Ava should be in the nursery."

"The nursery is currently empty of occupants, and when my brother's twins arrive, I would most likely move her out anyway for safety's sake."

"So it's true then what they say about the boys?" Devil spawn brats!

"I adore my family," Rebecca warned.

Adam bit his tongue. He hardly had a perfect child, but he was thankful Rebecca thought to protect Ava from her boisterous nephews. "If you think it best."

"I do," Rebecca began. "Now, let's get you settled upstairs, my lady."

"I'll come with you," Adam said quickly. While he was in that part of the house, he might be able to determine if his hope to visit Mrs. Warner's bedchamber one night was well and truly lost.

Rebecca seemed highly suspicious of his

suggestion but nodded. "Very well, if you must."

"Oh, I must." When Ava skipped ahead to the door, Adam pulled Rebecca near to whisper, "I'm still waiting for that invitation."

She stared at him. "Are you not forgetting something, my lord?"

Adam blinked.

"Your book? I should hate for it to be returned to my father's vast library by mistake."

Since Adam had not yet finished reading it, he would hate that, too. He turned back to fetch it and when turned around again, Rebecca and his daughter were gone without him.

He had to hand it to her, Rebecca was turning out to be a worthy sparring partner. He hurried to catch up.

Chapter Six

<hr>

Over the next week, Lord Rafferty proved to be a surprisingly good father to Lady Ava. He was affectionate, indulged her every now and then, and the girl did as she was told. Mostly.

Right now, Lady Ava was throwing sticks into the stream, as boys were often prone to do, and watching them float away. Lord Rafferty was helping.

Truth be told, Rebecca wasn't sure what to make of the earl anymore.

He was no longer flirting with her, but still dogging her steps whenever she stepped from the manor. He had been a perfect gentleman in every respect—which she found confusing. She had begun to think she had imagined his interest. "I must return to the manor soon."

"Oh no, just one more," Lady Ava cried, and rushed off into the nearby wood to hunt for fallen branches again.

"It's always just one more," Rafferty complained.

"You're the one letting her take advantage of you," Rebecca noted.

"She has no one else to take advantage of," Lord Rafferty stated as he joined her.

"You cannot make up for lack of mothering by spoiling the girl, or letting her run wild in those woods," she warned as she turned to watch the girl dart around the nearest trees.

"Trying not to," Rafferty murmured.

It had rained last night, and the hem of Lady Ava's skirt had become damp long ago. The girl would need to change into a fresher gown when they returned to the manor. Rebecca had assigned her own maid to look after the girl, since Lord Rafferty's summons hadn't brought one of his own. Rebecca had only heard good things about Lady Ava Croft from Nancy, which confirmed her own conclusions that the girl had excellent manners despite having such a father.

Rebecca felt a slight brush against the back of her hand and jerked it up to her chest, fearing an insect had landed on her. But there was nothing on her glove when she looked, and she forced out the breath she'd drawn.

"Lovely day," Lord Rafferty murmured, inhaling deeply.

"Rain on the horizon," she noted with a frown, hoping the dark, heavy clouds would miss the estate entirely. Parts of the celebrations were to be conducted out of doors.

Lord Rafferty began to laugh.

"What?"

"I knew you were going to say that," he promised. "I've never met a woman so keen to point out the hazards around them."

She put her hands on her hips to set the record straight. "If it rains, the roads will become more soaked and delay the wedding guests."

"Why is that a problem? The bride and groom really only care about tying the knot."

"We're still awaiting the special license Father promised Jessica."

"Ah." He held up his hands in surrender. "Fair enough."

"I do want my sister to marry."

"Of course you do," he said soothingly. Then he blew in the direction of the rain clouds. "Do go away, clouds."

Rebecca shook her head and looked away as Lady Ava burst out of the trees, dragging a large tree limb behind her. It seemed heavy, but Ava's eyes were fixed on the nearby stream. Rebecca clucked her tongue in disapproval. "I would prefer she not throw in the trees, my lord."

"So would I." He strode off, halted his daughter's plans, and then threw the branch over his shoulder, returning the thick limb to the woodland.

Lady Ava skipped toward her, grinning. "Father said I should stay with you."

"Did he now?"

"He said you could teach me how to be a lady. If I listened properly."

"That is often how it is done with any endeavor." The girl was sweet. Rebecca glanced down at Lady Ava, feeling a pang of regret. She enjoyed the girl's company but duty called. "I really must go back to the manor."

"We'll come with you," Lord Rafferty decided as he returned, brushing off his hands.

"Huzzah!" the girl cried. "We can have tea together."

Ava rushed ahead, darted this way and that as she explored the garden. Although Rebecca expected Lord Rafferty to forge ahead with his daughter, he fell into step beside her.

"Thank you for a lovely walk," he murmured.

Rebecca inclined her head.

There was a soft brush against the back of her hand again. She glanced down, and Lord Rafferty waved his fingers at her. "Caught me."

She stopped to stare at him. "What are you doing?"

"It's called flirting. Maybe you've experienced it before?"

"You're tormenting me. Annoying me. That was definitely not flirting."

"We each have our own opinions. What did Old Warner do to earn your admiration?"

Rebecca thought about that for only a moment. "We met, and he proposed."

Rafferty gaped. "And that was enough for you?"

"Yes, of course, it was."

"That is the most tragic courtship tale I've ever heard," he muttered. "Every woman deserves to be flirted with. Warner certainly cheated you."

Angered by the comment, Rebecca glared. "Thank you, my lord, for the reminder. I have firsthand knowledge of my husband's faithlessness, since I caught him in the act. I do not need you to rub it in my face."

Mortified by what she had just revealed, Rebecca headed toward the manor at a faster pace.

"Wait," Rafferty called out. "I didn't mean…"

But Rebecca would not stop. She was angry again, in a way she hadn't been in a long time. All his talk and false flirtations were cruel. She had been out walking on her own quite happily until Lord Rafferty and his daughter had joined her. Rebecca had even enjoyed the time they'd spent together until that moment. She would have been better served to stay in.

Rebecca heard screams and paused.

Lord Rafferty was suddenly at her side. "What the devil was that?"

When the screaming resumed, Rebecca grinned widely. "Nothing to worry about, I'm sure." She glanced at Lady Ava and regretted they must part now. "Don't let me spoil your outing with your father, Lady Ava. Excuse me."

She caught up her skirts and quickened her steps even more.

As she rounded the corner of the house, she saw a familiar traveling carriage on the drive and shook her head at the chaotic scene playing out before her eyes. Her younger brother Samuel stood beside the carriage, holding his twin sons by the shirt collars.

The boys were fighting to be free of the restriction and complaining very loudly.

They were also saying her name repeatedly.

"What is this ruckus about?" she called to them.

"Auntie Becca." The boys, suddenly released, sprinted toward her.

Rebecca dropped low as the boys flung their arms around her neck, nearly knocking her down to the ground with their enthusiasm. "My dear boys. At last, you've come."

Rebecca hugged them both tightly and kissed the tops of their blond heads. Rebecca had helped raise this pair of rascals for a few years after their birth before restlessness had driven Samuel from London with the boys in tow.

They turned their little faces up to hers. "We were in…" twin one began.

"Mupe Bay," twin two finished.

She cupped their tanned little faces. They did best in the outdoors, with few rules and space to run about. Cooping them up only brought out the worst of their natures. "Did you bring me any seashells this time?"

"We brought you…" twin two began.

"…something much better," twin one finished, burrowing closer.

"We brought you rocks from Dorset," Samuel told her as he strolled over to join them with a smile. "Ones with tiny leaves trapped inside."

She blinked.

The boys dug in their pockets and presented two very dull, flat-sided rocks to her, but as Rebecca squinted, she could make out the shape of some sort of fern leaf there. She could almost imagine they'd been drawn, sketched. "Leaves in rocks? Well, that is unexpected."

"They are both fascinated by our finds and couldn't wait to show you their treasures."

Rebecca nodded, brushing her hands over the boys' untidy hair. They were always excitable, and they were growing so fast. "I swear you've grown inches since I saw you last."

"Will you measure us?"

She ruffled their hair again fondly. "After dinner tonight, I certainly will."

"Auntie Jessie!" both cried out suddenly.

The pair shot away toward their other aunt, who had appeared from the shaded lawn across the garden. They were a whirlwind of excitement whenever they arrived anywhere. Later, when the novelty of new faces had ebbed, they would ignore everyone and get into the most trouble.

Rebecca straightened, knowing they would come back to her eventually for affection, and studied her brother carefully.

Samuel, her junior by two years, was still smiling. "Do I get a welcome, too, Becca?"

When he held out his arms, Rebecca hugged her little brother quickly. "You look very well, too," she whispered as her brother's arms tightened about her ribs firmly. He kissed the side of her head before releasing her and stepping back.

Samuel's face was as tanned as the boys, and his once short-cropped hair had grown longer and more unruly than it used to be. But it was the ease in his expression, the lack of discontent about him, that pleased Rebecca most. Samuel had lost his wife when the twins had been birthed and had never seemed happy since. Today, however, his eyes sparkled with excitement—the way they had when he'd been a boy and into as much mischief as the twins got into.

"A few months by the sea has been good for all of us," he confessed. "We met many odd fellows scaling the rock falls for prehistoric treasures. I felt right at home there amid the scavengers."

"I'm glad. I—"

"Are you not going to welcome me too, sister," an unexpected voice asked.

Rebecca looked past her brother's broad shoulders and spied their sister Fanny lurking behind him. Lady Fanny Rivers was fanning herself languidly but seemed not the least bit untidy after the journey with the twins. Rebecca always ended up very rumpled.

She frowned. "You came together?"

"We had some catching up to do." Fanny beckoned the twins near. "Children, come inside with me now. We must find their graces."

"Father is not here," Jessica said as she joined them. "He and the duchess went out in the carriage earlier today."

"We do not expect them back for many hours yet," Rebecca murmured.

"Ah," Fanny said, looking crestfallen. Fanny had been nearly impossible to be around upon learning their father had fallen in love again. Fanny had called Gillian Thorpe her friend first of all.

"Perhaps some refreshments," Rebecca suggested. "There should be tea and sandwiches and such in the morning room."

"That would be lovely until they come back." Fanny smiled smugly, the boys holding her hands now. "We will all be freshened up by then, won't we? The duchess and I have so much to catch up on. Come along, children. Let's get out of this dreadful heat."

The boys dragged their slow-moving aunt up the steps faster than she wanted to go. Jessica followed, hiding a laugh behind her hand. They reached the top of the stairs finally and disappeared inside.

Rebecca turned toward her brother and raised one brow. "What did she buy them this time?"

"A horse each," he answered with a jerk of his head toward the carriage. A pair of unsaddled mounts were being held by grooms near the carriage. The horses were quite tall and obviously of good breeding but they pranced with impatience. The boys were too young to appreciate such noble beasts.

Rebecca groaned inwardly. Fanny had too much money and often used it to get what she wanted. Apparently right now, she wanted to be the favorite aunt. "I suppose that bit of bribery might make them better behaved for a few hours."

"We can only hope. They still love their Aunt Becca best though," Samuel promised as he held out his arm for her to take.

The boys did not need more possessions. They needed the unconditional love and attention of their family. Rebecca laughed softly. "I wager you say that to all of us."

Samuel chuckled. "No, I mean it. They've really missed you most of all. We called at the townhouse in London first, only to be told you'd left for the country in something of a hurry. I trust nothing was wrong, or was the townhouse too quiet without us?"

"It always is." Rebecca did not tell Samuel why she'd fled London when she had or why she had planned to stay in the country so long. Like everyone in her family, Samuel would offer to fix her financial woes, and that would be embarrassing.

Samuel turned around and viewed the empty lawn behind them. "Was that Lord Rafferty I saw with you when we arrived?"

"Yes, he and his daughter are here for the wedding."

He threw her a grin. "Have you forgiven him then or can I expect unpleasantness between you still?"

"Forgiven him?"

"For climbing into your bed that one time?"

"For the last time, he climbed into an empty bed, before I had been offered the room, so it was hardly my bed to begin with." Rebecca shrugged off the gossip. "The tale is far more scandalous than the actual event was, I assure you. "

Samuel smirked. "A pity. You could use a bit of excitement in your life."

"My life is exciting enough as it is."

Samuel's eyes sparkled with mirth. "Oh, are you saying you have another admirer besides Rafferty?"

"You've been out in the sun too long, brother."

Samuel laughed then. "Well, if nothing else, the rumor that Lord Rafferty was rebuffed has likely given every other scoundrel reason to reconsider approaching you. The rumor gets more exaggerated every time someone talks about that night."

Yes, she had something of a prudish reputation thanks to that rumor involving Rafferty. She didn't mind if it kept scoundrels at bay, however, any man with honorable intentions had no cause for concern—not that she had noticed any lurking about.

They went up the stairs arm in arm and into the entrance hall, where Samuel greeted the butler as if a long-missed friend. Rebecca stood back, charmed by the exchange because she'd feared never to see her brother this way again. He was never proper, seldom considered his reputation or position in society and, like the sons he was almost raising singlehandedly, had boundless energy. He seemed to have finally found a measure of peace from his many travels.

As they moved deeper into the manor, they heard shouting ahead—familiar voices that would not be shushed. Instinctively, Rebecca quickened her steps. The twins had gone to the morning room with Fanny. They should have been amply distracted by the choices on the sideboard. However, the twins were not eating anything—they were fencing with chicken legs around Fanny as she did nothing to stop them.

Samuel rushed forward, complaining just as loudly, trying to put a stop to their antics, but the boys just dodged his outstretched arms, continuing the game.

Shouting at the twins never really worked and they'd obviously been shut up in a carriage for too long. Rebecca stood calmly, arms folded across her chest and waited to be noticed.

When they, at last, glanced her way, she whispered the twins' names in her steadiest voice.

Both boys froze, and they scrambled to her in a hurry.

She clucked her tongue. "What are your grandfather's chairs made for?"

"Sitting on," they replied with a grin.

She raised one brow, and they suddenly sank onto the edge of the same chair. "Much better. Now, where will the chairs you *can* stand on be placed?"

"Out on the lawn, so we don't hurt ourselves

when we inevitably fall off," they replied as one voice.

"Exactly. Let us not start this visit with either one or both of you confined to bed with a broken bone."

Both boys exchanged a long, silent look of horror.

"Now, let me remind you that the furniture in the manor is to be looked after properly. What is outside, in your area of the garden, is for play," she continued, noting that Fanny had settled in a chair—one closest to the door. "I want you to eat your fill of this fine luncheon while I make the arrangements for your amusements to be set up outside." She gave them a stern look. "No chicken leg sword fights in this room while I'm gone. Do you understand?"

They nodded very quickly, eyes darting to the nearby window. "Yes, Aunt Becca."

"Boys," their father said sternly, and their heads snapped around.

"We're really very sorry, aunts. Father."

"That's better," Samuel insisted. "Now eat so you have the energy to play later."

The boys fell upon the food as if they were starving at last. Keeping them in line was a full-time occupation. With the wedding and the expected guests, their father would not be able to spend every waking moment with them. Neither would she. They were such restless souls, much more so than any boys she'd ever heard of.

She stepped outside when she noticed her maid waiting. Nancy had been around the boys before and seemed unfazed by their antics. "Nancy, can you make sure the housekeeper is aware the twins are in residence and require their amusements to be set up as soon as it can be done."

"We can help too?" the younger of the twins offered, suddenly appearing at Rebecca's elbow.

"Indeed you can and will, Tommy. But not yet."

Rebecca drew the boy back into the room with her and urged him to sit and eat again beside his brother. Then she turned toward Fanny, who had collapsed into a side chair. "You must be fatigued from your journey."

"Indeed." Fanny was watching the boys with a wary expression. "I think I shall take advantage of the quiet to change before we meet the duke and duchess."

"Of course," Rebecca agreed wholeheartedly. "I'll have a maid sent to you as soon as possible."

Samuel covered his mouth and chortled as soon as Fanny was gone.

Rebecca tried not to laugh, too. "How did she survive the journey with them?"

"I never left her alone with them and I had the horses flank the carriage. The boys spent most of the journey with their heads either out the open door or with their faces pressed hard to the glass."

"Oh dear." Rebecca frowned, remembering Fanny's earlier comment about why she'd traveled with Samuel. "And what did she buy *you* this time?"

"Nothing I would accept."

Although curious, Rebecca did not press him.

When the boys seemed to have finished grazing on the food, Rebecca happily handed them over to a pair of strong-willed gardeners who could stand the shouting. "Enjoy yourselves, my dears. I'll be out to join you soon."

She stood at the window and waved them off.

Samuel joined her, munching still on a sandwich. "You don't have to mother them anymore, you know. They tell me they are quite grown up now."

"Grown up at six? Never. I always enjoy looking after them," she told him a touch wistfully.

A throat cleared behind them. "Lord Samuel. Mrs. Warner. Are we disturbing you?"

Rebecca turned around. Lord Rafferty again! His daughter was with him, so she had to smile. "Not at all. Do come in. Would you care for tea? A sandwich?"

"Nothing for me, thank you," Lord Rafferty said, but Lady Ava asked for tea. When Samuel and Rafferty strolled from the room, Rebecca helped Lady Ava chose a small piece of cake from the sideboard, too.

Rebecca poured tea for them both and sat down while the girl ate her fill.

Lady Ava glanced her way shyly. "Can I stay with you for the afternoon?"

"I'm afraid you would find my afternoon very dull."

When Lady Ava's face fell, she smiled kindly. "I am expecting a visitor very soon, actually. Someone about your age, too. Are you acquainted with Miss Olivia Hawthorne?"

Ava shook her head.

"Her father is a gentleman and they live not far away. Her mother is a good friend of the duchess'. She is one of six sisters, and I've invited her especially to meet you."

Rafferty returned to the room, smiling. "It was kind of you to arrange that. Thank you."

Rebecca considered the girl a moment longer. Lady Ava had changed into a lovely dress after their walk. However, it was not a dress meant to play in. "Why don't you run along up to your room and change into that blue spotted muslin you brought with you? Nancy will be happy to help you change if you ring the bell for her. I'll send for you as soon as the Hawthornes arrive."

Full of excitement now, Lady Ava hugged her impulsively then skipped out the door without saying a word of goodbye to her father.

Rebecca met his gaze, a little embarrassed

that she had managed the girl without his permission. "I apologize. I should have asked if you minded the connection first, my lord."

"You really do think of everything." He took Ava's place at the table. "I should apologize to you, too. My comment about your late husband was thoughtless and I am sorry if you were hurt by it."

"Accepted," she whispered, wishing he would leave it at that and go.

Rafferty stayed. "I've been wracking my brain all morning trying to think of ways to amuse Ava in the coming days. I do not mind the connection, but I only know the elder Hawthorne to look at. Natalia, isn't it?"

"Yes. Miss Natalia is the eldest of the six girls. Miss Olivia Hawthorne is about Lady Ava's age, she's the third child and has bookish tendencies." Rebecca smiled quickly. "She will not be a bad influence on your daughter."

"Good."

Rafferty captured her gaze and held it so long, she grew warm all over. Rebecca felt her body responding to that look despite her best intentions. She resisted the urge to shift position in her chair. She would not give him the satisfaction of knowing his flirtation affected her. It would only encourage him to grow bolder. "Where did Samuel go?"

"He didn't say where, only that he'd return by the dinner hour."

Rebecca frowned at the news. She had been hoping to spend more time with her brother. She hadn't seen him in so long. "Very well."

Rafferty's lips twitched. "What are you doing for the rest of the day, madam?"

"A great many things."

He smiled widely, undeterred by her lack of clarity. "Mind if I keep you company?"

"I do mind. You'll only distract me."

"That was the whole point," he said, and then chuckled softly. "But to make amends for upsetting you earlier, I'll leave you alone until dinner so you have no further reason to be cross with me today."

"Thank you," she said, relieved he would go away so easily and that he'd apologized.

Chapter Seven

Lord Samuel's twin sons ran past Adam the next day. A minute later, they both ran the other way. And so it went for the next half hour until Adam wished he'd not given up the drink. He had a hard time keeping up with the boys' comings and goings.

It didn't help that they seemed identical in every way—looks, clothing, even their hair was cut the same. Adam gave thanks that he only had one offspring to keep an eye on, and that she was occupied elsewhere right now.

The guests were milling about on the lawn, enjoying the pleasant afternoon and beverages laid out on a nearby table. Among the guests was Lady Morgan, a viscount's wife he'd known for many years. She caught his eye. Adam acknowledged her, and they drew together to speak. "Lady Morgan."

"Lord Rafferty. What a pleasant surprise to find you here."

He kissed her outstretched hand. Lady Morgan was a few years younger than himself. She was well connected and very easy on the eye. He considered her husband an excellent friend. "I could not miss such an occasion. Whitfield finally buckling under and giving up his bachelorhood. Who'd ever imagine such a thing?"

"No lady that ever tried to catch his eye," she answered with a soft laugh. "He's frustrated a great many of my friends over the years. As have you, my lord."

"Me? I was married."

"But no longer." Lord Samuel's twins barreled toward them, and Adam moved to protect Lady Morgan. The boys parted and ran around them, on their way to the far side of the garden. He stepped away from Lady Morgan as soon as the danger had passed. "It's a little hectic this year."

"So I see." The woman shuddered. "Now what was I saying? Oh, yes. It's past time you married again. You do need an heir, remember."

He shrugged. Adam would like a son but hopefully a quieter one than the pair circling the lawn right now.

"Come now. It's not like you to be shy when it comes to women."

"I'm taking a holiday." He glanced about the gathering and noticed an obvious absence.

"Where has your husband hidden himself? I don't think I've seen him since first breakfast."

Lady Morgan shrugged. "I suspect he's gone to the stables yet again to admire that pair of young geldings Lord Samuel brought with him yesterday. I think he means to make an offer, though I daresay he's gone on a fool's errand."

"We'll never know until he tries," he suggested. But Adam would wager that Lord Samuel would not sell horseflesh that had been a gift to his sons from their aunt. "How are your children?"

Adam's gaze fell on Lord Samuel's twins as they helped themselves to punch.

"Blessedly at home under the dowager's watchful eye. Oh, look at the mess they are making," Lady Morgan complained.

"Yes," he said. "My daughter is here this year."

"Yes, I saw her earlier in the hall with Mrs. Warner." Lady Morgan leaned closer. "You are to be commended, my lord. Your daughter is a delight. She reminds me so much of your late wife. So excitable."

Adam tried not to wince. "She's young yet."

"True." Lady Morgan pursed her lips. "Have you given any thought to employing a companion or governess to guide her education in the coming years?"

"She has enough servants at home."

"Country maids do not know how to

prepare a girl for securing a husband."

Adam looked at Lady Morgan in alarm. "She's barely ten years old."

"There is never enough time in a girl's life to learn all she needs before becoming a woman. The responsibilities of running a household and supporting one's spouse in their pursuits can be overwhelming for women of any age."

"I suppose."

Just then, Rebecca appeared on the lawn some distance away. She was alone. Adam hadn't seen much more than the back of her head for the entire day. She had been bent over her writing table earlier that morning, and Adam had paused at the doorway, hesitant to interrupt her work. He was pleased to hear that she'd spent a little time with his daughter. He had hoped for that.

What he wasn't pleased to realize was that Rebecca was barely spending any time enjoying herself or the party. For the life of him, he couldn't remember if in the past she'd been any other way. But the rest of the family had been having fun without her—strolling about the lawns and laughing together endlessly.

Rebecca glanced Adam's way once but continued on without stopping to talk. When she disappeared into the shrubbery beyond the gathering, Adam was intrigued. Did she not intend to spend one moment being idle?

Adam excused himself from Lady Morgan and followed after Rebecca.

He almost missed her at first. Rebecca had squeezed herself into a gap in a hedge.

He doubled back and stared. "What the devil are you doing?"

"Shh," she hissed. "You'll spoil everything."

Taken aback by her statement, he looked away briefly and spotted Lord Samuel's twins racing in his direction. They did not seem as if they would stop, so he sucked in his breath and raised his arms. They swept around him like the tide, excusing themselves, but raced on without stopping. He lowered his arms slowly, afraid they'd return at any minute.

A soft laugh reached his ears, and he turned. Rebecca eased from the shrubbery, flicking twigs and such from her shoulders and hair, but grinning. "I think your presence distracted them, Rafferty. Well done!"

"Are you playing hide and seek?"

She nodded. "Second time today. Do you never play games with Ava?"

"Tea parties," he confessed slowly. "It's a little embarrassing."

"Not to her. A little silliness now and then is good for the soul."

She brushed off her hands and turned to face the manor.

"Where are you going now?"

"I'm going back inside."

"That's cheating. Going inside is cheating," Adam protested.

"Well, no. Not exactly. We play by different rules than others might. The twins are given one chance to notice me, but if they don't spot me the first time they pass, I'm allowed to move to a more comfortable place. They know I'll return to my parlor eventually."

Strange game but with two active boys, he concluded it might be hard to play by ordinary rules. "If you know they'll find you, why not stay outside and enjoy the summer's day with everyone else?"

She shook her head. "I have a thousand things left to do yet, my lord."

He frowned at her now. "You're not enjoying the party you've organized, almost single-handedly it seems."

"Her grace needs to rest as much as possible, but please, do not tell my father I said that."

"He worries." Adam shook his head. "I thought you were avoiding me."

"Why would I do that?"

"You know why." He gave her a hard look and moved closer. The woman managed everyone very well but hardly gave a thought to her own needs. Not one member of her family seemed concerned that she was missing the party, either, but he certainly was. He studied her complexion. Fair and lovely. Perhaps she didn't like the outdoors. "Come back with me. I'll fetch you a glass of whatever you like and find a chair for you in the shade if you prefer."

"I'd rather not."

"A walk then."

She went to refuse, but he cut in quickly. "Isn't there something else outside that you must check on?"

She thought a moment. "I did want to know how repairs on the carriage were coming along."

"Well, there you go. We can walk to the stables together and you can check another item off those unending lists of yours. We can talk on the way there and back."

"Talk about what?"

He scrambled for a harmless topic and gestured her forward toward the stables. "Ava."

Her brow rose in surprise, but she fell into step.

"It was suggested I should employ a companion for the girl."

"You can, of course. Although…" Rebecca thought a moment. "She's a little young yet for a companion. An experienced governess would be a better choice."

"What should the governess be experienced in, exactly?"

She looked at him in surprise. "You're really asking my advice on how to raise your daughter?"

"Well, you've been on the marriage mart before. You've undoubtedly advised dozens of young women. You know what is expected during the season."

She blinked and then scowled. "Are you saying I'm old, my lord?"

He cocked his head. "You understood my meaning perfectly well, madam. Don't pretend to be offended that I noticed you're a little older and infinitely wiser than a shy debutant."

A soft laugh left her lips. Rebecca's whole face lit up as she fully absorbed his description of her. She should laugh more often, he decided. Adam had rarely heard Rebecca laugh, or ever given her reason to now he thought about it. She seemed a completely different woman when she was happy.

He absolutely had to delay her return to the house now. "Well?"

"Next spring is the earliest I would recommend hiring a new governess. Let her enjoy one more year without thinking about the future. Then a governess and a dancing instructor are essential before you should even consider which year to launch her into society."

"Good. Good. I have plenty of time then."

"However, it is not wise to be complacent with her education."

"I'm not!" he protested.

"She knows no French whatsoever."

Rebecca gave him a stern look. "She also has no friends her own age."

"She has friends at home," he protested. "And you arranged another for her yesterday."

"Friends whose parents are titled and also not tenants at your estate?"

"Ah, well, no. You are correct about that then. I only had the estate children when I was growing up."

"I had my sisters and brothers and made friends through those connections. But an only child, a girl, without siblings or a mother, needs a broader connection to members of the aristocracy."

"She seems to be getting along well with you."

Rebecca's expression grew amused. "If you're not going to take my suggestions seriously, my lord, I'll be on my way alone."

"Oh, no you don't. I'll escort you to the stables." They reached the stables soon after. The vast, sprawling building was teeming with activity at this time of day. "Wait here while I find someone for you."

He strode ahead, noting Rebecca had not disagreed with him for a change. He found the stable master and brought him back to Rebecca to question. It seemed the carriage would not be ready anytime soon. "I'm sorry, madam. There's a lot of work to be done yet."

"It's not your fault, sir. Thank you."

They turned back for the manor, but Rebecca seemed lost in thought.

"What's wrong?"

"Nothing," she said quickly. "I have to get back to my work."

He caught her arm. "You are making yourself a slave to your family."

She gaped at him in stunned silence. She swallowed. "I am not."

"I think you are. You're acting for the duchess in everything. This is your father's house, and he has a wife who should be arranging this wedding party."

"She's been very ill."

"Well, she's not today." He pointed in the direction of the guests he'd left behind. "Her grace is out there, sunning herself and laughing along with the rest of your family. So are your sisters."

Rebecca looked away.

"They are all enjoying an event you've slaved over for nearly a week now." He crowded her a little but lowered his voice. "Don't you think you deserve more than to become a servant to your own family?"

Her jaw firmed, but she did not argue with him. Rebecca seemed intent on making herself indispensable to the duke and duchess for some reason he couldn't fathom. The woman had her own life. She could also have a husband and children if she put her mind to it, too. She was meant for more than this.

"I see how you are with your family. You love them, that is obvious, but do they love you as much, eh? Where is the line drawn between doing what you think is your duty and enjoying a little independence from them? When are you going to put yourself first?"

She wrenched her arm from his grip. "You know nothing of my life."

"Well, I'm trying to, damn it." He drew closer. "You are the most irritating wench I've ever had the misfortune to find attractive. I'd seduce you right here in the garden if I didn't think you'd blame yourself for enjoying a moment of comfort in my arms."

Her brow furrowed as her jaw worked. Adam expected to be put in his place at any moment. He'd certainly hit the nail on the head. Rebecca Warner belonged in the spotlight, not in the shadows.

She nodded but then shook her head. "I beg you will excuse me, my lord. I have a game to return to, and that is not a duty, I assure you."

"Everything but pleasure is a duty. Oh, what the hell. I may never catch you alone again," he whispered.

He caught her face in his fingers, tilted her chin up, and planted a lingering kiss on her lips right there in the garden. He drew back slowly, saw the surprise in her eyes, and then kissed again for good measure.

She stared at him, lips parted and damp, for a full minute in silence afterward. He brushed his thumb across her mouth as he released her. "Now you know what might be yours if you just say the word."

When she did not give it still, Adam executed an elaborate bow, turned on his heel, and returned to the party.

Rebecca Warner hadn't responded the way he'd wanted her too. Perhaps she never would, but one thing he *did* know—Rebecca Warner was destined to be unhappy, and there wasn't a damn thing more he could do about it.

Chapter Eight

———◆———

Rebecca gulped as Lord Rafferty strode away in a huff.

Dear God, what a kiss!

She raised shaking fingers to her lips, painfully aware of the unfamiliar sensation of desire that still coursed through her veins. It had certainly been quite a while since she'd been kissed, and she was still in shock. She hadn't been prepared. She hadn't known how to respond to Rafferty at all.

Rebecca had never engaged in intimacies until after she'd married. Warner had never kissed her anywhere but in her own bed. After his death, she hadn't been courted again or even been seriously flirted with—not until Rafferty had singled her out so suddenly.

Feeling confused, Rebecca rushed back to the safety of her tiny corner of Stapleton Manor and shut the door behind her. Then, she found a chair and put her head in her hand.

What was she to do about Rafferty now? She had not asked to be kissed, she'd never encouraged him, and had done her best to ignore his bold flirtations.

But after that kiss, she couldn't understand why she had.

Admittedly, Rafferty was not a man she approved of in general. He was too loud, too drunk too often. Although, she had noticed he had consumed fewer spirits than usual.

But why on earth would he try to seduce her now?

As she sat there, in the grip of indecision, she heard an odd sound. The scrape of something being dragged along the floor behind her chair was all too clear.

She lifted her head slowly and turned.

Lady Ava, in the process of crawling across the parquetry floor, froze halfway to the door. The girl visibly shrank from her. "Hello," she whispered.

Rebecca sat up straighter. "Hello."

The girl licked her lips. "Please don't tell my papa that you saw me here."

Rebecca stood when the girl started toward the door again. "Stop. Stand up."

Lady Ava gained her feet, eyes wide and her lips trembling.

Rebecca approached her slowly. "Never let me catch you doing that again."

"I wasn't. I just…hid when you came in."

Well, obviously. "And you were trying to sneak away from me unnoticed on your hands and knees?"

The girl nodded. "Yes."

She sighed. "You will always be noticed. You are an earl's daughter. Come here and let me look at your gown."

The girl regarded Rebecca with resignation and moved to stand before her.

Rebecca quickly dusted off the girl's skirts. "There, that is better."

"Are you going to tell my papa?"

"I haven't decided." She put her hands on the girl's shoulders and made her sit down on the settee. "Why are you not upstairs at your studies?"

"Everyone is outside but me," the girl said in a small voice.

"Ah," Rebecca said slowly. She remembered what it was like to be left out of the games her brothers had played. But she'd always had her sisters to keep her company. "What do you normally do at home during the day?"

"I never have to stay in my room all day if I don't want to. I have a pony to ride, and I practice with my sword." The last was uttered very quietly.

"I did the much same as a girl," she confessed.

The girl looked at her with an expression of awe. "You fence, too?"

"I did once, but I grew out of it. My brothers taught me a little, and I learned the rest by watching them."

The girl wriggled forward on her chair. "Papa doesn't really like me talking about it, but would you teach me?"

Rebecca considered the girl and nodded slowly. "I have some free time after luncheon."

Lady Ava bounced in her chair. "Thank you! I don't know how I will be able to wait. You won't forget me will you?"

Rebecca wondered how often others had forgotten this girl and disappointed her. She reached out and brushed her hand over the girl's long hair. It should be tied up neatly to spare her the pain of knots forming. She needed a mother. Rafferty should have remarried years ago. "I'll collect you myself when everything is ready. I promise."

Rebecca turned as she heard the sound of footsteps rushing toward them. As they grew louder, she knew who was coming. She smiled, and a few moments later the twins wrenched open the door, scanned the room and then sprinted to be the first to touch her.

"We found you, we found you!" they

chanted. Then the pair grabbed her hands and tried to pull her away from Ava.

Rebecca resisted.

"Come on, Aunt Becca. We want to play again."

"Gently," she reminded them. "My dear boys."

But these were not her children. She could only love them until it was time to hand them back. Even though they desperately needed mothering, Rebecca wasn't the one that should. They were Samuel's responsibility, and one day he should remarry. She hoped he would soon. He wouldn't be alone then.

Not like she was bound to be.

Rebecca had trouble breathing for a moment as the truth hit her hard.

Rafferty was right. The choices she'd been making with her life would ensure she would always be alone.

Rebecca depended on herself and herself alone. She had relished her independence since becoming a widow. Rebecca could go anywhere, do anything, and say almost anything without having to account for her actions.

But it could be a very lonely life. She had made friends but sometimes friends were not enough. She had good reason to mistrust gentlemen, but when she did she was also denying herself the life she was born for.

Rebecca sucked in a sharp breath. She could

not allow that to happen, and there was no good reason she must remain alone for the rest of her life.

The children were watching her with a worried expression so she smiled at the twins and then smoothed their untidy hair one more time. "Why don't you pair go and find your father and ask him to play with you?"

"But we want you!"

"Not today, my darlings." She looked at Lady Ava, motherless and lonely—just as she was. They could be friends, as Lord Rafferty suggested, but that was not enough for either of them. It was time to stop hiding from the risk of being hurt.

The guests would be going in for luncheon soon, and Rebecca would be rejoining the party. She would enjoy herself—and see if the earl was truly interested in her. "I have somewhere I need to be soon."

The youngest of the pair eased onto her lap, pouting. "Are you tired of us like Aunt Fanny is?"

"Oh, never believe I could be tired of you pair of rascals." Rebecca pulled them to her and hugged them fiercely. "I will always love you both. Never doubt that."

She released them but grabbed their little hands. "How about we go and find your father together? Perhaps he can be persuaded to take you swimming. You still like getting wet, don't you?"

"Oh, yes. Yes!"

She gestured to Lord Rafferty's daughter. "Lady Ava, would you like to come outside with us?"

"Yes, but what will Papa say if he sees me`?"

She smiled. "I'm sure Rafferty will not mind just this once."

It took but a few moments to return to the garden, and as she predicted, the guests were stirring, ready to go back into the manor for luncheon. With the twins at her side, and Lady Ava following close behind, Rebecca weaved through the crowd until she found Samuel. He was talking with Lady Morgan, and she waited until she had his attention before speaking. "The boys are keen to visit the lake for a paddle."

Samuel exchanged a wry smile with Lady Morgan. "You don't have to tell me where you take them, Mrs. Warner. I trust you with them, always."

Rebecca shook her head firmly. "It would be better if *you* went with them."

Lady Morgan moved closer to Samuel, languidly fanning herself. "A paddle by the lake sounds very inviting, my lord. It's so warm today."

Did the viscountess intend to join them?

That wasn't what she wanted to hear. Lady Morgan was married. "Perhaps you could ask your husband to take you later?"

"But of course he can come with us," Samuel agreed.

The smile on Lady Morgan's face dropped away suddenly.

Rebecca almost laughed at the woman's change of expression. Her brother really should be more careful of married women with older husbands. Many became bored by the choices they'd made with their lives and looked to others for attention.

Samuel grinned. "The more, the merrier, I always say."

Rebecca eased back as the boys peppered their father with questions about visiting the lake and it became quite clear that their trip was imminent. She bid them an enjoyable afternoon together and turned for the manor.

Lady Ava's hand slipped into hers. "What can I do this afternoon?"

"Well," she began, but stopped when she caught sight of Lord Rafferty coming from the direction of the house. He seemed annoyed to see her, but then the expression vanished when he noticed his daughter. Rebecca approached Rafferty slowly, a little unsure of what to say to him now. She could not be rude to the first man who had wanted to kiss her since her husband's demise.

Lady Ava's hand slipped from hers when they reached him.

He stared at his daughter. "What are you doing outside?"

"Forgive me, my lord," Rebecca cut in before the girl could answer. "I thought Lady Ava might enjoy the party, so I stole her away from her studies."

His brow rose in surprise. "Is that right?"

"Yes, indeed," she lied.

Rafferty seemed unconvinced but shrugged. "Are you still playing games with the twins?"

"Oh, no. Not now. The children have taken their father to the lake, and they will all most likely paddle in the shallows until the sun is setting."

Rafferty glanced past her. "Not invited to go with them?"

She caught Rafferty's eye. "It was my idea for them to go without me. I thought it about time I joined everyone else."

Rafferty's lips twitched. "Done organizing us all then?"

"That is a chore that might never end, my lord."

"True." He turned to his daughter. "Back to the nursery for you, my girl. Your luncheon is waiting."

"Yes, Papa," she promised. "Thank you for

thinking of me, Mrs. Warner."

Lady Ava dipped into a curtsy and disappeared inside.

Suddenly feeling awkward, Rebecca glanced down. It wasn't a nice feeling being unsure what to say. Rebecca had no experience flirting with a gentleman.

Rafferty, however, seemed impervious to uncertainty. "Shall we go in together?"

She looked up quickly. "I'd like that."

"I know you just lied to me to protect Ava," he murmured after a few steps. "My daughter escaped all by herself, didn't she?"

"Don't be cross with her. She was lonely and could see the twins playing outside. Technically, she never left the house until I took her outside with me."

Rafferty grunted. "This is why I don't have another wife yet. I always suspected I'd be conspired against in any scenario involving my daughter's misdeeds."

She wanted to laugh but didn't dare. "Wives and daughters will tend to stick together."

"Do you remember your mother?"

She was surprised by the question. "Some things but not enough, really."

"Ava doesn't remember her mother at all," he admitted.

"She was very young when your wife died." Rebecca licked her lips. "Perhaps you should marry so she might have a mother again."

Rafferty choked and then coughed. "I've considered it but…these things cannot be rushed."

"True," she agreed. "It is a momentous decision to make a second marriage."

"Indeed."

They walked into the dining room together. Many were already gathered around the sideboard and took no notice of their arrival. "It is a buffet luncheon today, my lord, and you may sit anywhere you please," she told Rafferty.

"Excellent," he muttered before striding toward the sideboard, and the waiting servants eager to do his bidding.

Rebecca cast her eye over the gathering, noted all was in order, and then followed Rafferty, waiting her turn to be served. He did not acknowledge her and turned away to the dining table. Rebecca chose only a little of the food offered, and then turned toward the table, too.

Lord Rafferty had decided to sit in the single empty chair between Lady Morgan and Mr. Whitfield. Disappointed she could not sit next to him and continue their conversation, Rebecca moved to the opposite end of the table, where there was space for her.

Even though the food was excellent, Rebecca picked at her food. Lady Morgan's laugh reached her ears, and she looked up. Lord Rafferty was leaning toward the viscountess, clearly enjoying what she was telling him.

A little disappointed by Lord Rafferty's interest in Lady Morgan, a married woman, Rebecca looked away. What should she have expected?

For a moment she had started to like Lord Rafferty, but he was a scoundrel, and scoundrels had broad tastes when it came to women. She hadn't given him any sort of encouragement. Not the kind he must usually receive after a kiss, so he'd quickly found someone else to flatter.

A fog of perfume suddenly engulfed Rebecca as Fanny settled into the next chair. "Ah, there you are, Mrs. Warner."

"Lady Rivers," she said by way of greeting to her sister. She was not in the mood to spar with Fanny today. Fanny was popular, especially with unattached gentlemen.

They sat side by side, unspeaking for several minutes before Fanny leaned close. "Is that a scandal I see in the making?"

Rebecca followed the direction of Fanny's gaze to the other end of the table. The only possible scandal would be if Lord Rafferty tried to seduce a married woman and succeeded. "I don't see anything."

"Of course you do. I think marriage has finally begun to bore Lady Morgan. How exciting for her."

Rebecca's eyes widened with alarm. "Don't say that."

Fanny shrugged. "Why not? Oh, I know you disapprove of women engaging in discreet affairs, but not all of us dislike men the way you seem to."

Rebecca looked at her sister in surprise. "I do not dislike gentlemen."

Fanny sipped her wine but her expression was assessing. "My dear, your scowl gives you away every time some poor man is nice to you."

Rebecca's cheeks heated with embarrassment and she quickly looked around. "I do not scowl that much. I'm thinking," she insisted.

Fanny chuckled softly. "You were always so serious when we were young. I'd hoped that might change. At least we will never compete for the affections of the same gentleman ever again."

"What?"

"Oh, come now. There's no need to pretend any longer. I know you wanted River for your husband from the moment you met him."

Rebecca gaped. "That is not true."

"Rebecca dear, it was obvious to all that you were crushed when he proposed to me instead.

Things haven't been the same between us since."

Rebecca set down her fork. "How could you believe that? I wanted *you* to marry him."

"Is that why you made sure to dance with him at every ball? I don't think so."

Rebecca turned in her chair and gripped her sister's arm urgently. "Yes, I may have danced with him often, but it was so I could decide if I liked him enough to consider him a worthy inclusion to the family. If he weren't a decent man, worthy of marrying you, I would have informed father straight away."

Fanny appeared skeptical but then clucked her tongue. "No one has ever asked you to interfere in our lives. And did we stop you marrying your choice? No, we did not."

Rebecca sucked in a sharp breath of shock when she spotted Lady Ava peeking around the doorway across the room. The girl ducked back out of sight quickly but Rebecca was sure she was still there hiding. She glanced around the table but no one had noticed, least of all her father. But he was still busy flirting with Lady Morgan.

"I don't care what you do anymore," Rebecca said absently, keeping watch for the girl.

Her father would not be pleased that she had disobeyed him a second time that day.

Fanny sighed. "Oh, don't get in a huff."

Ava poked her head out again, and when she waggled her brows, Rebecca choked on a laugh.

Everyone at the table looked at Rebecca but, to her relief, Ava had already slipped out of sight.

Rebecca had laughed because the girl had looked so much like her father that it had taken her by surprise. She glanced at him and caught him looking away from her.

Fanny nudged her arm. "What was so amusing?"

"Oh, nothing important."

That girl was going to get them both into trouble. Rebecca really didn't want Rafferty to yell at Ava today, so she quickly bid her sister goodbye and went to find her.

Once outside the dining room, she looked everywhere for the girl. Eventually, a servant asked if they could be of assistance. "I seem to have lost sight of Lord Rafferty's daughter. She was right here a moment ago."

The servant gulped suspiciously.

"Where is she hiding?"

He pointed behind her—at the servants' staircase.

Rebecca entered the staircase, let her eyes adjust to the dark, and found the girl backed against the opposite wall. She held out her hand for the girl to take. "If you won't do as you are told, you will come with me."

She took the girl down to the servants' quarters. The great kitchens were bustling with activity, and she did not distract them by making any requests. She found the keys to the wine cellar herself, collected a candle and unlocked the door. She slipped inside, pulling the girl with her. "Here we are."

"I don't like it here," Ava said immediately.

The room was cold, cavernous and every step they made echoed. Rebecca hadn't been down here in years.

Ava nearly clung to Rebecca's skirts as Rebecca searched the dark corners for her stored possessions, but eventually, she found what she wanted—a long wooden case hidden under a bundle of discarded sacks. She opened the box and grinned. "I think this might change your mind. Look."

She took out a padded vest, one worn for protection, and showed the girl what was underneath.

"Is this yours?"

"Yes, I was about your age when I last wore this vest. Father insisted I needed protection from my brothers." She took it back and helped Lady Ava don the garment, buckling the straps firmly. "What do you think?"

The girl spun about in a circle as if wearing a pretty new gown. "It's perfect."

Then Rebecca slipped her fingers around

the hilt of a small tarnished sword and showed the girl that, too.

"It's not made of wood. It's just my size!" Lady Ava cried.

Rebecca nodded. "It is only to be used for practice."

She handed Ava the weapon by the hilt.

"She's wearing protection, but you are not, Mrs. Warner," Lord Rafferty warned from the open doorway. "Are you sure that is wise?"

"Papa, look at me!"

"I'm looking." While Lord Rafferty and his daughter admired her padding, Rebecca found the old practice dummy leaning against one corner of the room and dragged it to the middle of the open space.

Ava was quick to join her. "What's that for?"

"Practice dummies do not bleed like your father or I will."

Ava approached the dummy and struck it once, awkwardly. "Like that?"

"No. Here, let me show you how we do it at Stapleton."

Rebecca took possession of the weapon, recalling the instruction she'd been given as a child. She wielded the little sword a bit awkwardly at first but soon got a feel for the blade once more. She advanced on the dummy and then danced around it, striking as often as she could.

Lady Ava was right. Swordplay was invigorating—at any age, too.

When she stopped, Lord Rafferty clapped. "Now that was a performance I would have paid to see."

A little flustered by the compliment, Rebecca handed the girl the weapon. In her renewed joy in the sport, she had forgotten she had an audience. "It will take practice, but if you apply yourself, you might one day be competent enough to face a real opponent."

"Let us hope not," Lord Rafferty muttered.

She glanced his way and noticed an odd smile on his face.

That man. Perhaps it was his size, but she couldn't look away. He was broad in the chest, more substantial than most men in every room. He had attractive features, he wasn't pretty, but he seemed assured. Confident. Perhaps that's what she noticed most of all about him.

He drew closer. "One of these days, you and I will have to engage in swordplay."

"Do you think I haven't the skill to take your blade, my lord?" she asked.

He choked, and Rebecca suddenly realized what she'd actually said had a scandalous second meaning. She closed her eyes briefly, and when she opened them again, Lord Rafferty's expression was utterly delighted.

He advanced a step to whisper, "I know you

can take me." His lips quirked. "But we'll never know how well we fit until you invite me to your room. Tonight?"

"Did you see me, Papa?"

Rebecca whipped around, horrified she'd forgotten the girl could be listening. "You were wonderful," she promised quickly.

"Yes, wonderful," Lord Rafferty agreed, moving past Rebecca with a sigh. "How about you give your papa a turn with that little thing."

Rebecca shrank back into the shadows but kept her gaze on Rafferty as he moved.

He was still interested in her, but she had a lot to lose if he was discovered in her bedchamber, or seen leaving it later. The respect of her family was important to her. She could not throw out her morals simply for one night in Lord Rafferty's arms without considering the future. But Rebecca couldn't deny he tempted her.

Chapter Nine

———◆———

Adam looked up as the door to his bedchamber creaked open just a bit—and then he was utterly dumbfounded to see Rebecca Warner dart inside. The door shut quietly behind her, and he stood still in shock. What the devil was Rebecca doing traipsing about the manor house in her nightgown or coming into his room at this time of night?

There must be something wrong. "What is it? Is Ava all right?"

"Your daughter is fast asleep already," she assured him in a whisper. "I made sure she was before I decided to come see you."

He drew closer, noting Rebecca appeared anxious, wringing her hands before her. She was dressed for the bedchamber—her hair tied in a loose plait that draped forward over her shoulder to her waist. "If not Ava, then what is wrong?"

"Nothing is wrong, my lord."

"Then why are you here?"

Rebecca remained by the door a moment, her eyes large and fixed on his, but then she took a single step in his direction. "I thought… You offered to…" she began, and then clamped her lips together.

He'd offered to share her bed, but she hadn't invited him. He'd phrased his offer many different ways, and he'd definitely been understood. He'd kissed her and received no reaction to that, either. Certain he'd failed, he'd made one last attempt that afternoon but Ava had spoken, and he hadn't been alone with Rebecca since.

Had he been entirely mistaken about his chances? Had Rebecca been thinking about his suggestion all this time and only now found her courage?

Adam ran his eyes over the woman again, liking what he saw very much. Her body was hidden beneath yards of soft white muslin and lace, but that didn't diminish her appeal. He could hardly believe that the prim and proper woman had come to his bedchamber dressed like that—or for the purpose he hoped. "Are you here for *me*?"

Her head dipped quickly into a nod.

He had underestimated the woman—she might feel just as lonely as he did, but she was not confident of what she was doing. That much was evident in her nervous mannerisms now.

"Welcome then," he murmured, and then slowly advanced on her.

Rebecca held her ground, but he could see her panic clearly. She was breathing too fast, and she wasn't looking him in the eye as she usually would. He'd rather not have Rebecca in his bed if she was going to regret it afterward. "I know what I said to you was shocking. I'm a direct man, and I do want you. I didn't expect you to take such a risk with your reputation by coming to me this way."

"I would rather it be this way," she whispered, and then looked up. "There will be no misunderstandings between us after."

"You do realize you will not be able to claim you didn't desire me, don't you?"

She nodded. "You will not misunderstand my intentions, either. You do not own me. After tonight, we will never speak of this again."

He frowned at her request. As a young man, he'd tried to avoid entanglements with lovers who'd expected a commitment. But he was older now and valued women more than he once had. What if he wanted another night with Rebecca? It wasn't outside the realm of possibility that he would still desire her in his bed come morning.

But if she said no, then it was no, and he

would not argue. If she changed her mind after tonight, he would not tease her for it or refuse her. "No one should own anyone," he promised. "Come here."

And she would come many times during the night if he had his way, too. Something about the prickly Rebecca had always gotten under his skin. He wanted to do indecent things with her. He needed to make her scream, make her moan and beg to come undone again and again.

She took a step toward him and stopped closer than she usually would dare in public.

She was a small thing, every woman was small compared to him, but her eyes were fixed on his chest, and her sharp intake of breath seemed quite loud in the quiet room. He watched the play of emotions on her face. He had already begun undressing for bed. All he had on was his shirt, sleeves rolled to his elbows, and a pair of thin unmentionables clinging to his hips.

He wondered when was the last time she'd seen a man without breeches. "I can hardly believe you are here," he whispered, brushing his fingertips across her warm cheek.

Her brow furrowed. "If you did not want me here, I can go."

"I like that you came to me this way, but I never expected you to. You seemed...almost impervious to seduction. I have spent a great deal of time trying to figure you out."

"When you weren't deliberately provoking my temper," Rebecca accused.

He grinned, thankful he'd given up spirits for the house party. "You have a fine temper. Very easy to rouse. But I guarantee I will give you no reason to complain about me tonight."

She sighed. "Must you always talk about what you want?"

"Yes. If I were a quieter man, more prone to introspection than action, you would not have come to me."

He reached for her plaited hair and untied the ribbon that held it together so neatly. When he had it, Adam waved it before Rebecca in triumph.

Her eyes widened slightly. "Give that here."

"No," he said as he tossed the ribbon away. He worked quickly to free her hair. "Now is not the time to be neat or tidy, madam."

There had always been tension between them. Tonight that tension would turn into a blistering passion, Adam hoped.

He slowly glanced down her body, taking his time to peruse her attire, and found another bow to tug on. Rebecca Warner came wrapped as a gift just for him. He captured the end of the little ribbon and loosened it, too.

Rebecca's breath came faster now, pushing her breasts into prominence, and he was glad for her reaction to what he was doing. He slowly peeled back the sides of her robe, exposing her prim nightgown beneath. Yet another example of proper ladylike attire. She was modest, in and out of bed. Rebecca was destined to be a wife one day—no doubt about it.

He set his hand at the small of her back and pulled her closer. Rebecca swayed but resisted a little. He moved them, circling around to put himself between her and the door, and then when he was confident he had her full attention, he began to shift her backward subtly toward the bed. Towards the place where he would finally find out if Rebecca's salty tongue was good for more than tearing strips off a man.

The moment she bumped into the bed, she turned her back on him and tried to scramble up onto the vast mattress. But before she got too far away, he caught her robe and gently drew it down her arms and off.

Rebecca moved onto the bed wearing just her nightgown—her slippers had apparently already been discarded somewhere along the way, because her feet were already bare.

When she was seated on his bed, eyes fixed on him, Adam discarded his shirt slowly. He stretched out one hand for her to take then brought it to his face.

Rebecca's hand was warm as she hesitantly caressed his skin.

Adam caressed her face, too, and moved his fingers to the edge of her mouth. Her jaw softened, her face relaxed while he played with her bottom lip, urging her lips to part.

He bent forward slowly, and at last pressed his lips to hers properly.

Rebecca yielded with a small moan, leaning back and drawing him down over her.

Adam was only too happy to comply, but he would not be rushed. Rebecca had soft lips of course, and he was soon swept away by the feel of her mouth moving under his. These were no missish little kisses, though. Rebecca held nothing back.

She swept her tongue into his mouth first, catching him by surprise, making him reassess the slow pace he had believed he should set with her.

He cupped the back of her head with his hand, filling his palm with her soft hair, and slowly covered her with his body. She regarded him with unblinking intensity, offering up no words of encouragement whatsoever. But her hands grazed his chest, twirling across his skin with maddening gentleness.

It was so good to be in a bed with her that Adam forgave her lack of conversation. She wanted him, and that was all the encouragement he needed to make love to her tonight.

She drew him down for more kisses, hesitating only long enough to rearrange her nightgown higher and widen her legs. She urged him between her thighs, and then her knees cradled his hips. Adam pressed his body against hers, feeling the warmth of her skin heat his. The neediness, the insistence of her kisses inflamed him. He put his hand between them, found the drawstring on his unmentionables and, once loose enough, shoved them down past his hips.

The moment he felt her hands slide across his back, he knew that there would be no stalling, no other conversation, no hesitation, either.

He ran his hands along her soft thighs, found his way under the bottom of her nightgown and wriggled his fingers along her body. He closed his fingers over the rounded curve of her derriere and squeezed.

Mrs. Warner moaned against his mouth as he kneaded her flesh but she did not stop kissing him; she pressed her sex up against his erection impatiently.

The woman was nothing like he'd imagined in bed. She was coming undone quite swiftly, and there was no way he would risk disappointing her by not giving her what she seemed to desire most.

He found her sex with his fingers, slid through her curls and found moisture. She lifted her hips into his touch eagerly. Adam pressed two fingers into her tight body, and she writhed against him—forcing them deeper inside with every movement. Adam set his thumb gently to her clitoris and exerted a little pressure.

Rebecca gasped softly, and her eyes squeezed shut as she rocked back and forth.

It was heaven to be with a woman who got straight to the heart of what she wanted in bed. Rebecca was very wet, and his fingers stroked through her slick folds smoothly. Had she been thinking about him since his very first invitation or even before that? He'd love to find out one day.

He drove his fingers inside her again and again, pushing her passion higher, but it wasn't enough for him. He longed to feel her body close about his cock. To have her come apart around him. He replaced his fingers with his cock but pushed in slowly, basking in a sudden burst of restrained cries of encouragement from his lover. Her back arched when he sank fully inside—and then he lost himself in making love to a woman who asked for so little.

He loved Rebecca hard, fast, and much longer than he thought possible as she dug her nails into his back and wrapped her legs about his hips and spurred him on wordlessly. She turned her face down into his shoulder.

All that was left was for her to give in.

But not like this.

Adam caught Rebecca's hands and raised them above her head. He laced their fingers together as he slowed his strokes. Her eyes rose to his, and he thought he'd never seen a more beautiful woman. Rebecca's hair was tangled about them in lovely endless waves. Her lips were pink, flushed from his kisses, but it was her eyes that captivated him. They glowed with so much passion that it nearly took his breath away.

Pinned to the bed, Rebecca was utterly bewitching to behold—and all his for one glorious night.

He worked himself in her body, determined to keep a steady pace until at last she found her release. Her eyes squeezed shut, and her body arched up to his with delightful agility. Rebecca was exquisite, more passionate than he had counted, more willing than he'd ever assumed. Rebecca was such a contradiction, he was momentarily overwhelmed with tender emotions he'd never expected to feel again.

He loosened his hold on her hands and lowered himself until her still-clad breasts brushed against his chest. He caught her mouth with his and kissed her soundly, and then he withdrew to surrender to pleasure by his own hand.

Adam muffled his groan against her hair, and then slumped as her arms wrapped tightly around his neck, keeping him close. He savored the long moments Rebecca held him, too. Affection after had been unexpected.

Before he really wanted to, he rolled over,

wiped his sticky hand on his discarded shirt and threw it away.

He fell back to the bed and drew Rebecca to him, draping one arm around her heated body. He relished the feel of a soft bundle of gentle warmth against his skin—a balm for his lonely senses. Another unexpected pleasure.

Rebecca seemed happy enough to remain with him longer, too. She sighed deeply, burrowed close and then grew still. Minutes ticked by, and still they said nothing to each other about what they had done. But his mind was whirling with plans for a future that did not include never talking about making love to Rebecca again.

He'd pleased her. He was sure of that. There was no reason not to make love to her again if they both wanted more.

He glanced down at her face. In repose, she seemed as grave as ever. But he'd never think of her that way again. Yes, she was serious, but she made love like a wicked angel.

Could he hope for more, tonight or any other night to come? The last house party the duke had thrown had lasted for weeks, and it would be delightful to be together as many times as they liked.

He could be discreet. He could pretend that nothing had changed between them in front of others for as long as necessary. He stroked his fingers down Rebecca's spine and back up. Yes, another night with this woman was what he desired most.

Rebecca shifted suddenly, and he was filled with panic that she might leave already. But her face lifted to his, and he saw a question in her eyes.

"Stay," he begged softly. Adam almost didn't recognize his own voice. He'd never wanted a woman more than he did Rebecca at this moment.

"I'd like that," she whispered. She subsided in Adam's arms again, but her hand landed on his stomach.

Her soft touch drifted slowly over his chest and then started to wander much lower. She circled his naval several times before Adam moved onto his side to face her.

His cock was growing thick again thanks to her wandering hands, but he ignored his own needs to rouse hers again. He reached for the buttons at the top of her nightgown and undid a few.

Rebecca sucked in a breath of surprise as Adam moved his hand until it settled over her bare breast. Definitely a perfect handful. "You are so lovely," he told her before pressing a kiss to her brow, and then another to her temple.

"Shh," she whispered back. "You talk too much."

"Not when it's the truth. You're a lovely and exciting woman."

Her fingers traveled downward slowly and

brushed against his thickening cock. She glanced down and captured him. He moaned, and Rebecca laughed softly. "Are you really as insatiable as you seem?"

"Oh, much worse. I'm going to make love to you again and again and again. Till dawn wakes us."

Her lips found his then, and she pressed her body against his urgently. Adam wrapped his arms about her, determined to make good on his promise.

Chapter Ten

Rebecca rushed towards the Duke's study the next day, eager to answer the unexpected summons. She had been deep in conversation with the duchess about some last-minute arrangements she'd made for Jessica's wedding day, happily handing over all further responsibilities for the upcoming nuptials. The duchess had assured Rebecca that she was well enough to take over. She'd been so grateful and had made an embarrassing show of trying to thank Rebecca. Thanks had not been necessary. What she had done was out of love for her family.

She tapped on her father's study door, letting herself in at his entreaty to join him.

Her father was alone, standing beside a window reading a letter.

"You sent for me?"

"Yes, come in, Rebecca," he said slowly. He folded the letter and studied her with a frown.

Rebecca came to a stop before him. She did not like the way he was looking at her. She worried that he knew about her and Rafferty somehow. "Is something wrong?"

"Yes. I have a letter of yours."

She smiled in relief. "A letter of mine?"

He lifted his hand. "In any other circumstance, I would apologize for my mistake of opening a letter addressed to you, but I cannot today. Why didn't you come to me?"

"About what?"

Father handed her the letter. "The letter is from your solicitor. How long has this been going on?"

Rebecca scanned the letter quickly. It was her expected quarterly statement. An accounting of available funds from her jointure and also of investment income received too. But there was a note mentioning an expense she'd questioned last quarter, which is what concerned her father. Mr. Barclay reported the problem solved. "There is nothing going on."

"The people who manage your money should not make any mistakes."

Rebecca folded the letter, noting the paper carried the scent of Barclay's horrid snuff. Father was wealthy enough to hire a dozen men to keep accurate records. Rebecca's funds did not stretch that far. "It was just a simple mistake. I wrote to him immediately and as you just read, he has made the correction."

"Damn sloppy," Father complained and then his eyes narrowed on her. "What else haven't you told me?"

Rebecca sighed. There were many reasons she hadn't confided in her parent—his unexpected marriage, her sister's first season, the distance that had always existed between them. She lifted her chin. "Nothing, I swear."

"I'll write to my secretary in London and have him locate you a competent employee to keep your accounts in order."

"I prefer to deal with my solicitor myself."

"Damn it, girl, you could be facing financial ruin if this continues."

Rebecca looked Father in the eye. He was behaving exactly the way he always did. Exaggerating a problem to disaster proportions when it was anything but. "It is an uncomfortable situation when a mistake is made, but I have no fear for my funds."

Arguing with Father rarely solved anything to Rebecca's satisfaction. Perhaps she should return to London briefly soon and consult with Barclay before Father took it upon himself to interfere in her life.

Father had folded his arms across his chest. Not a good sign. "Since you are so concerned, I will return to London after Jessica's wedding and arrange a meeting with Mr. Barclay."

Father held out a silencing hand. "I'll come with you."

Rebecca shook her head firmly. "You are needed here. For your wife's sake, I will not accept your company. You shouldn't leave the woman you claim to love when she is carrying your child. You cannot abandon Gillian."

Her father frowned then, and she saw she had at last found a logical way to curb his meddling. He claimed to love the duchess and hesitation proved it was true. She waited for his reluctant nod and hid her smile when he gave it.

"That is settled then," she said briskly, intending to withdraw.

"If only Warner were alive, he would handle this matter for you," Father called out. "You were much too young to be widowed."

Young perhaps, but she was no longer mourning. She could not mourn someone who had never really loved her. She turned back. "If Warner was still alive…" she mused, and then shook her head. "He would have assumed the debt was mine and that I was lying about it."

Father appeared shocked by that. "Surely not if he had the facts."

Rebecca shook her head. "My marriage wasn't that way. I always had to account for every penny spent and bargain for everything I needed."

Father took a step forward. "You never said you were unhappy."

"I wasn't. Not in the early days of the marriage. But Warner betrayed me, and then he was gone. I am independent for the first time in my life, but it has taken a long time for me to feel comfortable again. Even now, spending money is hard for me. Because of him, I've kept every bill, recorded the location of every purchase I've ever made since becoming a widow."

Father drew close. "You should have told me."

She smiled for his sake. "I didn't want to worry you."

"Child, I have worried about you since the day you were born," he promised, unexpectedly drawing her into his arms and embracing her. "It is foolish of you to think I could stop now."

Rebecca hugged him back and her eyes filled with tears as he kissed the top of her head. Father was not as affectionate with her as he was with her sisters, but she always believed she had his love. When released, Rebecca stepped away from him quickly. "I can take care of myself now."

Father sighed. "I see there's no stopping you but should you run into any problems in the future, I want your word you will at least tell me what is going on. I'll believe you, no matter what."

She wouldn't send for him. "Yes, Father. Thank you."

Impulsively, she kissed his cheek, and then fled his presence.

Stapleton estate was now back in the hands of its rightful mistress, so with nothing else to do, Rebecca fetched her bonnet and set off for a walk alone in the sunshine.

Rebecca had not had very much time to herself lately. She'd hardly had any fun, except for the children and meeting with Lord Rafferty last night. A walk to the lake and back would clear her head, and then she would return to enjoy what was left of the party.

Father's estate was well-tended, as all ducal estates should be. The servants in the gardens lifted their caps when she passed, but she did not stop until she could see the lake ahead.

Her eyes landed immediately upon Lord Rafferty. The earl was standing with his back to her, taking in the same view.

She had enjoyed surprising him immensely last night and had appreciated the bedroom skills he had so boldly boasted of lately. She felt satisfied with their coming together, pleased that he had comported himself as a gentleman in bed. There had been no awkward moments between them or lack of attention bestowed on her. She had been thoroughly bedded during the night and had achieved satisfaction on both occasions. Indeed, Rafferty may have wanted a third tumble this morning. However, dawn had been approaching, and she'd been eager to return to her own bed unnoticed.

They had not spoken since.

Rebecca cleared her throat and descended the short slope to meet him. "Good morning, my lord."

Lord Rafferty turned around, his eyes widened a little when he saw her coming toward him, and then he quickly removed his hat. "Good morning, Mrs. Warner. What an unexpected pleasure to see you here."

There seemed to be no undertone of seduction to his welcome, merely a polite courtesy exchanged between acquaintances. Rebecca took the remaining steps towards him and then dipped a curtsy. "And you."

His smile grew. "What are you doing wandering alone on such a glorious day?"

She allowed her eyes to roam over his big frame for a few moments before speaking. Again, Rafferty was wearing one of his terrible waistcoats. It was too much to expect him to change but Rebecca had to admit that after last night, she might prefer him without any clothes on at all. She swallowed down her scandalous thought quickly. "I was getting some fresh air and exercise."

"Yes, the drawing room seemed quite stuffy

this morning. You missed nothing of any note. Just a bunch of windbags gossiping about people they think they know."

Fanny had been holding court in the drawing room. "A good reason to be outside. Where is Ava today?"

He smiled. "Ava has been invited to the Hawthornes to visit, and I have graciously allowed her to go without me. I trust she will behave herself."

Rebecca had seen the two girls together and was pleased with their similarities. "I think we will avoid disaster. What are you doing out here alone?"

"Pondering improvements. Would you care to join me on my stroll about the estate?"

She liked that they were not awkward with each other and nodded. "I'd enjoy that."

Lord Rafferty held out his arm for her to take, but she declined.

"I am quite capable of walking on uneven ground unaided."

"Just trying to be a gentleman," he promised with a laugh. "I did not actually expect you to take my arm, but I offered it just the same for the sake of good manners."

She frowned at him. "You're making fun of me."

"Did you think I would not seek ways to provoke you just because we spent the night together?" He leaned a little closer. "If anything, I think you can be assured of an increase of teasing after such an exciting night."

She blushed. "Is there really a need to speak of last night?"

"Yes, but only when we are alone," he promised. "If the inclination strikes you, I would be most happy to have your company in my bed again."

Rebecca tried to hide her smile. She might visit him again but she would not give him advance notice. "I would not assume any such visit is guaranteed."

"You cannot blame me for attempting to coax you back into my bed. I much prefer kissing that pretty mouth of yours instead of being lashed by it. Not that I dislike our arguments exactly," he promised. "A little verbal sparring can be quite stimulating in the right setting."

"Is that right?"

But then Rafferty cursed softly. "I'm afraid we will have to continue this at another time. Your sisters are coming our way."

"Damn," Rebecca muttered under her breath, too. She'd been avoiding Fanny for years, and she'd done enough for Jessica to last a lifetime. She hoped not to speak about the wedding again until the day arrived.

Rebecca smiled when her sisters drew close

but she'd rather they went away. She'd been feeling very good since she'd woken this morning. She didn't want her family to spoil her pleasure in the day or her time alone with Rafferty. "Good morning, Lady Rivers. Lady Jessica."

"Mrs. Warner. Lord Rafferty." Fanny offered Lord Rafferty a smile as Jessica linked her arm through Rebecca's. "What a surprise to find you here together."

"Simply out stretching my legs." Rafferty pointed ahead, where another couple walked together. "Everyone seems to have had the same idea this morning, too."

"We must join them," Fanny insisted. She held out her hand to Rafferty, and he offered his arm.

The pair walked on ahead.

Jessica drew Rebecca along behind but at a slower pace. "We thought to save you," Jessica whispered.

"Save me? From what?"

"Everyone knows you and Rafferty do not see eye to eye."

Rebecca pressed her lips together. She disliked Rafferty when he was drunk and disorderly, which had not been the case today or for the past week. He seemed to have mellowed despite his suggestion that he could not change for any reason.

Lord and Lady Morgan greeted them with great excitement, Rafferty particularly. The Morgans were not her particular friends, but she noted the pair seemed keen to monopolize the conversation. They talked of parties they'd all attended recently, and made plans to meet at amusements Rebecca would not usually be invited to.

Feeling out of sorts about that, she wet her lips and pasted on a smile.

But then Lord Rafferty caught her eye and offered a small smile of his own.

A short, small burst of pleasure washed over her skin, causing a blush. "I think it's time for me to head back to the manor," she murmured quickly before anyone noticed her reaction to the earl. "Enjoy your walk."

"Yes, until later," Lord Rafferty agreed.

But then Rafferty was suddenly at her side, falling into step with her.

She gulped. "What are you doing following me?"

"I'm not following you," he argued. "I'm continuing my walk. We just happen to be going in the same direction for once." He laughed and then pointed ahead. "But first, there's something over there I need to ask you about. Hurry. I promise it will only take a moment of your time."

"Very well," she agreed reluctantly. Rafferty

had said he was considering improvements he could make to his estate. She followed him into a vine-covered walkway. "What is it? This?"

"No, this." He turned suddenly, looked around them, and quickly captured her face in his large hand. "I'm kissing you."

He bent his head and brushed a sweet kiss on her lips.

Rafferty drew back and waggled his eyebrows the way Ava had just yesterday. "Just a taste of what could be yours again tonight."

Despite her annoyance with him for the trickery in getting her alone, she laughed. "You, my lord, have a one-track mind."

He nodded and drew closer. "You'll get used to me. I'm an acquired taste"

He stole another kiss that had Rebecca swaying on her feet. "Stop that," she chided. "Or I'll go."

His answer was a cheeky grin. "That reminds me, I've been meaning to ask what brings you to the country so early this year?"

She looked at him in surprise. "I always stay at my father's house during the summer."

"But you never arrive in May," he said. "Usually you stay in London or attend a house party until June at least. You always bring that blonde woman with you, too."

She did not want to discuss her falling out with Charlotte. "Not this year."

"So when and where is the first amusement you will attend after your sister's wedding?"

Rebecca frowned. "I haven't accepted any. Why do you ask?"

"I think the next one will not see me kicked out of your bedchamber."

Rebecca turned away. The earl was making it very plain that he wanted more than she'd ever considered to give him, but an affair or series of discreet meetings with a gentleman had never been what she'd anticipated for her life. She wanted more than that. Respectability. A place in society.

None of which Rafferty seemed ready to offer her.

"You were drunk," she reminded him, turning back. "Let us not talk about the future today."

He stroked her arms briskly. "As you wish, but don't think I will stop trying to lure you back into my arms."

She spotted guests coming in their direction and took a step back. She pointed at the structure above them. "So, the garden arch is about fifteen years old," she told Rafferty in a voice sure to carry well across the garden. "The vines were planted the spring after its construction."

"It's lovely," he agreed, half-laughing. "I have one just like it at home, but it's not as old as this. You'll see what I mean when you visit."

Visit? Rebecca forced a smile but her happiness in being with Lord Rafferty diminished. Lovers were temporary, and they were never, ever to be confused with having honorable intentions. Until that moment, she hadn't really thought their affair could be more, but she suddenly wanted a new life. One with a husband and children of her own.

She bid Rafferty goodbye and returned indoors.

Chapter Eleven

"Are you not drinking again, Rafferty?" Lord Samuel Westfall asked as he appeared at Adam's elbow.

Adam considered the dregs of his whiskey he'd been holding for the last hour and decided he wanted no more of it. He was not in the mood for alcohol. Not when there were much more exciting things to do in the evenings—namely, finding a way to get near his lover of last night again.

"Not in the mood," Adam murmured, offering up a smile but keeping a sharp eye on Rebecca's movements about the drawing room. Right now, she seemed intent on organizing her family yet again.

Adam had become fascinated by watching Rebecca flitter about the drawing room, coaxing everyone to enjoy themselves. She was good at getting other people to do what she wanted without them ever realizing that she had. Rebecca had a talent for organization; for bringing people together, too.

"I'll have to drink the best Stapleton has to offer all by myself at this rate," Samuel complained. "Father may have mellowed because of his marriage but has outdone himself with this house party."

Adam looked at Lord Samuel in surprise. "You should have directed that compliment toward your own sister. Mrs. Warner's to thank for the success of the house party. She's been working tirelessly for a week and more."

Samuel's glance was assessing. "Is that so? She never said."

"It's her way, isn't it?"

Samuel chuckled softly. "We started calling her the general after Mother died."

Adam nodded. So her managing skills dated back to that point in her life. Adam raised his glass to his lips and contemplated his unexpected lover. With the youngest sister, Lady Jessica, Rebecca was openly affectionate. But with her other sister, Lady Fanny Rivers, Rebecca seemed to hold herself apart. There was little warmth or approval when they looked at each other. Even with the Duke of Stapleton, Rebecca was far more reserved than the others. She seemed closest to Samuel and his twin sons.

Adam hadn't had a good reason to contemplate the Westfalls in any detail before now, but after the last days in Rebecca's company, he was keen to know her better. Who better to question than her favorite sibling?

"How long are you staying at Stapleton?" he asked the man.

"Not too long. Never do. The boys are restless souls," Lord Samuel advised with a nod.

Samuel's twins were a pair of rascals with everyone, except their aunt Rebecca, who seemed to turn them into absolute angels with just one glance. They did what they were told for her. They were quiet for her. They looked to her for approval. The love she bore them was touching and also sad in a way. Rebecca doted on them in a way that had Adam imagining her with her own child.

"Your boys seem quite fond of their aunt."

"Oh, yes. Can barely keep them apart when we're in the same house. Just this morning they escaped the nursery early to wake her and say good morning. She's so good with them."

"She should have her own family to chase about," Adam mused.

"Agreed." Samuel nodded sagely. "But I dread the day she marries again."

"Why is that?"

Samuel's jaw firmed. "It's so easy for the boys to wear out our welcome. Warner never wanted any of us around really."

"Oh, I see," he said. Family was important to Rebecca. She would want her brother and the twins to visit her in any home she lived in. Adam liked Lord Samuel already and the boys—well he'd grow accustomed to them over time. "I'm sure you've nothing to fear."

"Your girl has impressed my sisters with her pretty manners. They'd steal her away from you if they could," Samuel told him with a laugh.

"I'm glad, but I assure you, my daughter is wanted at home. They cannot keep her." However, he was not opposed to sharing his daughter's affections. Rebecca had given him good advice already, and he hoped to hear more soon.

When he looked around, Adam spotted Rebecca standing at the hall doorway with his daughter beside her. Ava seemed unusually agitated, and Rebecca was trying to placate her. Ava should have been in bed at this hour. "Do excuse me."

He made his way to meet them. "What are you doing downstairs, young lady?"

"I have a letter," Ava exclaimed, waving a bit of parchment about. "My very first from a friend! See, it is addressed to Lady Ava Croft from Miss Olivia Hawthorne."

"She's very excited," Rebecca explained. "The footman should have given it to you first.

I've already spoken to him."

"Let me see that." He made a show of inspecting the letter, read the prettily worded thank you for visiting from the Hawthorne girl, and smiled. "I see you made a good impression."

Ava beamed. "Can I invite her to visit us straight after the wedding?"

Adam glanced toward Rebecca and caught her tiny nod encouraging the idea. Going home was not in Adam's immediate plans, though. "I'll think about it," he answered evasively.

"But Papa," Ava complained, "I already promised to let her ride my pony. She doesn't have one."

Adam held up his hand to stop the flow of words. "It is late, Ava, and I will need to consult my appointment book before you can reply. I'm sure the girl can wait for an answer for one night. Her mother will understand."

Ava's face pinched with worry. "How long are we staying at Stapleton?"

He glanced at Rebecca and felt his heartbeat quicken. He would stay as long as he could manage it. He was not done with Rebecca Warner.

"Your father has given you a reasonable answer, my lady," Rebecca told Ava in a soothing tone, taking over. "Your father is a great man, with many responsibilities."

Adam couldn't help but puff out his chest a bit at her praise. "We'll talk about it soon," he promised. "Now, shouldn't you already be in bed?"

"Yes, Papa."

Ava may have agreed, but she sounded so disappointed, Adam softened. "Would you like me to walk you up?"

"Mrs. Warner has promised to tuck me into bed tonight," Ava told him, but then a worried frown appeared on her face as she looked between him and Rebecca. "Is that all right?"

"It is. Please don't let me delay you," he murmured. The quicker Ava was safely tucked into bed, the sooner Adam was free to be alone with Rebecca. He'd kept a distance since their kiss in the garden, determined not to give them away. Rebecca was quite particular about keeping up the appearance of propriety at all times.

Adam's heart lightened as the pair bid him good night and moved upstairs together, holding hands. Rebecca seemed a good influence on his daughter, and Ava appeared to like her, too. Ava had had little to do with women beyond his own household and his own family, comprised of old aunts who pinched Ava's cheek and gave terrible advice.

He returned to the drawing room, mingling with the duke's family and guests. But the one face he really wanted most to see, the one person he felt most drawn to, was Rebecca Warner. The woman who was currently mothering his daughter upstairs.

Adam sighed, accepting that he would have to wait his turn for a little of Rebecca's attention.

Whitfield strolled up and pulled him aside. "I'm off to bed."

Adam grinned. "The last peaceful sleep of a single man."

Whitfield shook his head. "What are you going to do when I'm married, Rafferty? You'll have to find someone new to torment."

Adam had already found someone. He was well ahead of Whitfield's suggestion. He might even want to keep her.

He had singled out a suitable candidate to marry without even realizing what he was doing. He saw nothing to hinder the match. She was a duke's daughter without a husband, and he was a rich earl in need of an heir.

Finding the right time to broach the subject might be tricky, though. Ask for her hand too soon, and Rebecca would say no immediately. Too late, and she might think him an irredeemable scoundrel.

Adam nodded slowly. Yes, Rebecca Warner might just do for him as a wife and for Ava as a mother, if she wanted the job.

He smiled quickly at Whitfield. "I'll wake you

at dawn, so you're not late to the ceremony."

Whitfield chewed on his lip a moment, and then his skin colored pink. "Perhaps it would be best if I come to find you, instead," Whitfield suggested. "To avoid any awkwardness."

Adam almost laughed out loud. He'd already suspected the wedding was mere formality between Whitfield and Lady Jessica. It was the way they looked at each other that gave them away. He'd wager they were already spending every night together. "Understood."

Whitfield moved away, made a show of wishing his future wife good night, before appearing to depart the manor for his neighboring estate.

Adam watched closely and in less than five minutes, Lady Jessica was declaring herself exhausted, too.

He kept his amusement to himself as she left the room, no doubt intent on a pre-wedding assignation with her betrothed, and found an out-of-the-way spot to observe his acquaintances.

Most were married, half happily.

Yes, Adam would like to be married again. To have Rebecca host a gathering of their mutual friends like this at Gable Park, and when it was all over, they could slip away together.

Yet, he hadn't the faintest idea if Rebecca

might consider him a potential spouse or even want to marry again. She seemed to have a full life chasing her own family about. She spent most of her time living in their homes.

He would have to pick the moment he broached the subject very carefully if he wanted the best outcome.

Shivers tickled the back of his neck, and he glanced around suddenly, catching Mrs. Warner observing him from across the room. Although she tried to hide what she'd been doing, Adam was utterly charmed by her blushes.

Determined to speak to her, he made his way across the room. She met him halfway.

"I trust my daughter gave you no trouble?" he asked immediately.

"Not at all, Lord Rafferty, although she was very wound up over her letter still."

"I think I will issue an invitation to the Hawthorne girl, but as you suggested earlier, I should not let Ava immediately believe she'll have everything she asks for."

Rebecca beamed. "Very wise, my lord."

"Yes, you are wise, my dear," he murmured.

She nodded but looked around. "I trust you have enjoyed your evening."

"Indeed. It has been an exciting house party so far. I hope to enjoy the delights of Stapleton Manor for days to come."

Her face became closed off, and then she smiled benignly in a way he instantly knew meant he's said something wrong. "We should expect very fine weather for the wedding tomorrow."

"And for the wedding night, too, I trust?"

"Yes." Her lashes fluttered and she looked away. "You will have to excuse me, my lord. I see my maid trying to catch my attention."

Adam donned a concerned expression as he reached for her hand. "May I escort you to her?"

Rebecca allowed him a brief hold of her hand before pulling it back and looking beyond him. "I don't think so."

Adam was certain no one at the party had the slightest inkling that he and Rebecca had shared a bed, but he could tell that Rebecca lived in fear that someone would uncover their dalliance. If he was going to marry her, Adam had better start behaving like a suitor soon, or Rebecca might think him only interested in bedding her.

Winning her complete trust might just be the greatest challenge of his life.

She would make a perfect countess, but he knew precisely why he'd not thought of her before. She was not sweet. She was not even particularly friendly. She was argumentative, disapproving of Adam's drinking. Slow to change—her father had warned him of that one.

Yet, Adam found Rebecca wildly appealing despite all that.

Rebecca knew everybody he knew. She knew precisely the right fork to go with the right plates, the right dishes to serve at a lavish wedding. She was beyond painfully organized. Those were not skills they shared. Adam was spontaneous, optimistic and frank.

She was none of those—except when they had been alone together.

Rebecca had once complained that he was a degenerate drunk with no sense of decency. He'd deserved that set down because he'd stumbled into a bedchamber meant for her use. For years, he'd used the drink to keep him company.

Never again would he need to if he married her.

He leaned close to her and whispered, "Dance with me?"

She looked so startled he had to smile.

"Dance with me tomorrow at the wedding."

"You don't dance."

"I used to," he admitted. "I haven't felt the need to in years."

Her brow creased with a frown. "Have you been drinking again?"

He didn't blame her for the question. He'd

been playing the drunk for so long, she couldn't yet see the change she'd wrought. "No, and I'm still waiting for an answer, madam."

"I don't mean to dance at all tomorrow night," she told him. "I'm sorry."

"Damn but you don't make it easy for a man," he told her, but he could see her face had set into frost once more because his voice had become louder. How was he supposed to woo her if she refused to accommodate such a harmless request? Men and women danced together all the time and it meant nothing. No one cared about one single dance. Two, though, and people might whisper. "Make no mistake, I'll be back tomorrow night when the dancing begins to ask you again to stand up with me."

He bowed to her and stalked off to cool his temper. In the past, he would have headed straight for a bottle. But he would not fall back on old habits yet. Her lack of ease around him in public was a small setback. One he would overcome with her. One day.

He groaned out loud, and then turned on his heel and took himself to bed. Alone again and doubly frustrated. There was nothing to be gained in remaining in the drawing room if he couldn't talk to her.

He was inside his room only ten minutes before the door opened and closed behind him.

Rebecca had followed him. "What is wrong with you?"

"Wrong with me? Everything—and it is your fault."

Her brow furrowed. "I don't understand. I thought you said you were enjoying your evening."

"I wanted to enjoy it more, with you by my side." He raked a hand through his hair as his frustration exceeded his patience. "You are so afraid someone might see us together and leap to conclusions you constantly deny me your time."

"Have you no care for my reputation?"

"Of course I care about that, but I wasn't about to seduce you in the drawing room. Promising to dance one dance with me does not necessarily amount to shouting that you've had me."

"Shh," she warned because his voice had risen.

"Yes, I'm well aware that you live your life expecting the worst. I, however, do not."

"I have a lot to lose," she warned.

"And so much to gain if you could just trust me a little."

"I trusted a man once," she complained bitterly.

He advanced on her. "I am not Warner. I never once strayed in my marriage. I would not treat you so poorly."

She looked up then, eyes huge with emotion. "How can you be so certain? Men have urges."

Adam shook his head, quite willing to kill her late husband all over again for what the bastard had done to Rebecca. She appeared confident, assured, but she was plagued by insecurities. "My urges, as you put it, lie solely in one direction. What of yours, Becca?"

She lifted her chin proudly. "Do I really have to say it?"

"Yes, sometimes a gentleman likes to know how a lady feels about him—from her own lips," Adam warned.

She made a grumbling sound. "Well, I'm not going to flatter you and say that last night was the best of my entire life. I'm sure you could tell it was."

"No, I didn't realize that. Tell me what you liked about last night? Specifically."

Rebecca fidgeted under Adam's gaze. "I don't know," she wailed suddenly. "I don't know how to say the things you want to hear. Other women—"

"I don't give a damn about what other women might say or do with me. I want *you*," he whispered. He caught her head and pushed her body against the nearest wall, leaned down until their lips were inches apart. "If you won't tell me what you feel, how can I know what you want from me? I have yearned to get my hands on you since the moment we met by the lake today. Our kiss was too brief to satisfy me, and every moment since we parted then has been agony. That is what I think and feel, madam."

Her eyes grew wider than ever. "Agony?"

"Agony," he insisted. "So close but so far out of my reach. I ache for you," he admitted.

Rebecca licked her lips. She stared at him for a long time before answering. "And I for you."

She suddenly stretched up and pressed her lips to his. Adam bent his bigger frame to fit hers, and then put his hands beneath her sweet derrière. He lifted her up against him and, using the wall to support more of her weight, he ravished her mouth.

Rebecca wound her arms around his neck and held on to him as if she wouldn't let go.

Adam quickly hiked up her skirts until they were bunched about her hips and he squeezed her bare backside, reveling in the small moans she let herself utter.

Rebecca's hands were suddenly all over him, tugging at his clothing. Adam held them a little apart so she could unfasten his breeches, and when he felt the last button pop, he shoved the garment down his legs.

He pressed against her again and kissed her

soundly.

The sensation of his hard cock against her bare skin was heaven. Rebecca trembled in his arms, rubbing her body against his urgently and kissing him more hungrily than he thought possible.

She broke away suddenly. "I need you."

Adam knew where.

He wrapped her legs securely about his hips and brought one hand between them.

He teased Rebecca, and she gasped and shuddered in apparent ecstasy at his touch.

Adam wrapped his hand about his cock and rubbed the tip back and forth across her clitoris. "I love the way you move against me," he whispered into the shell of her ear.

His confession earned Adam another small shudder and another throaty moan from the quiet woman. Adam set his lips to her neck and nibbled, devoting himself to making her moan over and over.

Rebecca loosened her grip on his neck suddenly and slid her hand between their bodies. The tips of her fingers brushed against the head of his cock a few times, but then she dislodged him completely.

Adam drew back to see what she was doing, and his cock thickened even more. Only Rebecca's hand remained to tease herself with now, but her thighs were still wrapped tightly around him.

He moved to enter her, brushing the head against her opening. Then he pushed in to the hilt, straight and true, and claimed her body for his own. Rebecca's eyes fluttered shut, and a small smile turned up her lips. When he withdrew, Rebecca was quick to sink herself against him again.

Adam had not intended the night to begin this way, but he couldn't stop now.

"Please," she begged. "Faster."

Adam complied. He made love to Rebecca until the portraits hanging nearby rattled with every thrust. He loved her until he was panting and desperate for release. Her fingers tangled in his hair and she pulled hard, whimpering her pleasure.

Adam kept his attention on her face now, and he slowed his pace. The lamplight showed every emotion there was to see. "I want to see you come for me."

She parted her lips, and then her fingers fluttered over her sex once more.

She writhed against him desperately. Adam kept his thrusts even and waited for her to climax. Her body suddenly clenched around his cock and a small sob left her lips as she shuddered. Her body shook around him again and again, and she buried her face in his shoulder as the spasms continued to wrack her body.

Adam was overwhelmed by her pleasure. He slammed into her once, twice, and then he loosened his seed inside her.

Panting hard, they stayed together, gasping as one for several minutes. Rebecca's sex still twitched around him as Adam hugged her tightly. He swept her hair from her damp face and nuzzled her lips gently.

He eased from her body and then swept her into his arms. Adam had to shuffle to the bed because his breeches were around his ankles, but he managed to set her down on his sheets without incident. He undressed her carefully in silence, and then pinched out the candle. He stripped and slid into bed beside her in the dark.

Adam drew Rebecca into his arms. "You are an incredible lover," he told her.

She put her hand on his chest and looked up into his face. "I think you are, too."

Adam grinned. "Finally a little flattery."

Her face clouded with remorse. "I don't mean to be cold," she whispered. "It's just I've never once had to talk this way. It isn't proper."

He kissed the top of her head quickly. "I guess I'll always know when I've pleased you and when I don't. I hope you'll always tell me that you are satisfied."

"I am," she whispered.

Tomorrow, Adam would begin his campaign to turn that *I am* into an *I do* as soon as possible. He had not been in control of his passions enough and if he got her with child, her reputation would be in tatters. It had not been intentional but she would hate him for that.

He snuggled closer to her and covered them with a sheet. It was a warm night, and Rebecca fell asleep in his arms very quickly. Soon after he was very glad she had. A group of people passed his door. Any earlier, and they would have heard he and Rebecca making love. They had not been quiet that time.

Chapter Twelve

———— ◆ ————

"Weddings are such bittersweet occasions, aren't they, sister?" Fanny murmured as she and Rebecca stood back while the younger sister finished being dressed for her wedding. It was almost time to go down, too. Gideon Whitfield must be growing impatient.

The most anticipated occasion of the summer had everyone at Stapleton Manor smiling. From the servants to the many guests, the manor house was buzzing with enthusiasm. The flower-strewn drawing room was already filled with visitors who had made the journey to be with the family.

Every corner was festooned with ribbons and bows, and the great mantle, above which now hung the portrait of their late mother, stood in readiness for the ceremony.

Rebecca was content. She had done her

part, made sure her sister's special day would be as memorable as possible.

But tomorrow morning at first light, Rebecca would leave for London.

"She looks lovely," Rebecca murmured, full of love for her younger sister. Jessica was marrying a man who truly loved her. And although at times Jessica was a little overwhelmingly attached to Gideon Whitfield, Rebecca believed that their match was perhaps the best she'd ever beheld. It was undeniable that Gideon adored Jessica, and that was all Rebecca could ask for.

Fanny hugged Rebecca suddenly. "Are you thinking about your wedding day like I am?"

Rebecca hadn't thought of her own special day very fondly in years. She didn't want to spoil today with introspection that could only leave her feeling bitter. She pushed the memories away. "Yours was such a grand occasion."

Her sister made a little sound. "I remember hearing about yours after the fact."

"You and Lord Rivers were in the north at the time," Rebecca reminded Fanny. "You had been away for so long."

"I would have come back to see you like this," Fanny murmured. "I should have been with you."

Rebecca shook her head. "I really don't want

to dredge up the past today of all days."

Fanny sighed. "We should thrash this out soon. You are my sister, too, and I don't like that we don't talk about anything important anymore. I'm sorry about what I said yesterday. I thought, I assumed, incorrectly that you were jealous."

Rebecca shook her head. "I only ever wanted you to be happy in your life with Rivers."

Fanny sighed. "I wish Rivers had lived a little longer. There was so much we wanted to experience together. He was so fond of Jessica, and of you."

"He was a good man." Rebecca sighed.

"The same could not be said about Warner. He wasn't evil, but he was weak and too used to having his own way in everything."

Rebecca crossed her arms over her chest. *So much for leaving the past in the past.* She'd much rather think about the present. The future was too uncertain to be relied upon.

"What do you think, Mrs. Warner? Is she ready to be given away?" the duchess asked Rebecca as she stepped back from the bride.

Fanny rushed to Jessica and caught up her hands. "I couldn't imagine a more beautiful bride."

Rebecca shook her head. "Something is missing."

She went to a nearby table and opened a

drawer. She had thought of a surprise for Jessica days ago, and the duchess knew all about it. She removed a stunning hair comb from the drawer, one crusted with sapphires and diamonds. It had belonged to their mother but was now part of the new duchess' collection of jewels. Each of them had worn it during their own wedding ceremonies.

Rebecca approached her sister with it, holding it flat on her palm. "Mother would have wanted you to wear this today."

Jessica's eyes filled with tears and she placed trembling fingers upon the heirloom. "I thought you had forgotten the tradition."

"Never, my darling."

Rebecca moved behind Jessica. She gently inserted the precious jewel into Jessica's hair and then tilted her head a little so she could see it in the twin mirrors she stood before.

The duchess beamed. "Now you are the perfect bride! Your mother would be so proud of you today." The duchess dabbed at the corner of her eye suddenly. "I'm certain she'd be crying like I am about to."

"Our mother did love weddings," Rebecca agreed.

Jessica worried her lip. "I'm afraid to move my head. The piece is not too formal, is it?"

"Absolutely not," Fanny gushed. "You honor our mother by proudly wearing her jewels."

Jessica's lips trembled, and Rebecca rushed forward now before she burst into tears. Practicality had its uses. "Let me see you. All you need now is to pick up your flowers and to walk downstairs with Mother and Father by your side. After all, we can't trust you not to sprint into Gideon's arms."

The duchess choked on a laugh. "That's what I was afraid of, too."

Jessica laughed along with them. "I wouldn't embarrass him or any of you like that." She smiled impishly. "But you can't stop me running to him after I'm married."

Rebecca laughed along with the duchess and Fanny. "Come along, Lady Rivers. We must leave so Papa can steal a few minutes alone with the bride."

Rebecca opened the door and discovered Father pacing outside. "She's ready."

"At last," he exclaimed with a grin. He went in, and Rebecca closed the door to give them privacy. Although Fanny tried to linger to listen in, Rebecca was having none of that and pulled her sister away firmly. "Neither of us need to hear or see our father burst into tears again."

Fanny gaped. "Did he cry on your wedding day?"

Rebecca stopped in her tracks and nodded slowly. "Didn't he with you, too?"

Fanny frowned now. "No! He told me he loved me and would miss me, and that was all he said."

Fanny had always been close to Father. Closer than Rebecca had ever been. She glanced at the closed door they'd just left and her eyes stung. She had assumed she wasn't his favorite child for so many years, it was disconcerting to realize she hadn't missed anything of her father's love. "He told me it wasn't too late to reconsider."

Fanny caught her arm. "You have to tell me all about it. Was it embarrassing? Did anyone else see him do it?"

Rebecca smiled quickly. "Some other time. I don't want to miss a moment of the ceremony. We had better hurry along to join the guests."

They slipped into the crowded room and separated. Fanny went right and Rebecca to the left. She had promised to stand with Lady Ava for the ceremony.

The girl seemed relieved to see her. "You look so beautiful."

"Thank you. Not long now," Rebecca promised, and then placed her hands on Lady Ava's shoulders to hold her still.

Rafferty noticed and nodded his approval. "She's a little excited, I'm afraid."

"I've never been to a wedding," Ava confided, looking up at her.

Rafferty nudged the groom. "Almost time."

Whitfield looked a little wild about the eyes when he turned around to view the gathering, and Rebecca's grin widened. The poor man seemed worried when there was no reason to be. The harder parts of marriage came later.

Lady Ava wriggled closer, and Rebecca put a restraining arm about her shoulders. "Be still now. I don't want to miss a moment."

At some signal from the door, Rafferty propelled Whitfield toward the vicar.

When Jessica appeared on Father's arm at the doorway, a collective sigh swept through the room. Father's eyes were thankfully dry, and Jessica's smile was unrestrained as she approached her future husband.

When Jessica and Whitfield met before the vicar, Rafferty stepped back to stand beside Rebecca. She glanced at his waistcoat, pleased to see he had chosen to wear something more appropriate today.

Seeing Jessica about to marry the man she loved instantly swept Rebecca back in time. She was reminded that her own wedding day had been a much quieter and more somber affair than this. She had been a nervous bride, especially so after her father's outpouring of emotion. She had almost cried, too, but the marriage had been expected for her. She'd done her best to secure the right husband but failed.

Jessica was undoubtedly the lucky one. She was not nervous at all. She'd live close to her family for the rest of her life.

She felt a touch against her fingers, and since no one could possibly see it, she allowed Rafferty to hold her hand during the ceremony because she suddenly felt the need for support. Rebecca had married a severe man who had exhibited great reserve in public. It was only later that she'd discovered his flaws and the selfish scoundrel he really had been. She would not make the same mistake the next time she married. If she married anyone, they would have to prove they could put her needs first.

Rebecca nodded as the happy couple completed their vows.

And then it was done. The last Westfall was married. The bride and groom exchanged a chaste kiss then turned to face their well-wishers.

Rice suddenly rained down over the pair, and Rebecca enjoyed Whitfield's shocked expression. "That was my idea," she told Rafferty.

"I like how stunned he looks," he admitted as he let go of her hand.

Rebecca waited her turn to congratulate the couple impatiently. She addressed her first words to Whitfield. He was her new older brother, after all. "Congratulations, Gideon, and welcome to the family."

He leaned forward to kiss her cheek. "Thank you, Becca. My dear sister."

She smiled, congratulated Jessica with a kiss to her cheek, too, and then moved back so others could speak to the happy couple. She collided with Rafferty almost immediately. "A beautiful ceremony," she murmured after apologizing for not noticing him.

"Indeed it was. For a moment there I thought Whitfield might actually faint."

"He's made of sterner stuff than that," Rebecca promised, smiling down at Lady Ava, who was grinning madly. "After all, he is related to the Westfalls now. Westfalls do not ever faint."

"I'll keep that in mind."

Rafferty's hand settled at the base of her spine briefly. "Where to next?"

She shivered. "Drinks in the garden so the dining tables can be set up in here."

"I'll help encourage everyone outside, shall I?" he offered.

She nodded, pleased to have his assistance. Dealing with society was akin to herding cats sometimes. "I will circulate with Lady Ava then send her back to the nursery?"

"Please do," Rafferty murmured. He kissed his daughter's head. "I will come for you just before the wedding breakfast begins. All you will miss is boring talk."

"All right," Lady Ava grudgingly agreed.

Rebecca took up the girl's hand so they didn't become separated and led Ava around the local guests. She introduced the girl to a few people she should know already by now but didn't. Ava charmed everyone she met and seemed to soak up every word Rebecca spoke about her. By the time they reached the hall, Rebecca was very sorry they had to part. She handed the girl over to her own maid, who'd come down to peek at the wedding, too. "Leave her in that dress but cool her face, please."

"Yes, madam," Nancy promised before taking the girl away.

A servant hurried toward her, appearing quite agitated. "Excuse me, madam."

"What is it?"

"A visitor is waiting to speak with you in the Peach Drawing Room. I'm afraid they are not on the guest list."

"A visitor. Now? Who?"

"A Mr. Peter Warner presented his card just as the ceremony began and demanded to see you. I put him off until now. What shall I do with him?"

Rebecca gasped. She was expected back inside for the party, but she could not neglect her brother-in-law. She hadn't spoken to Peter Warner in over two years and had no idea what he might want with her. "I will see him. Would you inform her grace that I have been detained by a member of my late husband's family? Tell her I will return as soon as I can but if I don't appear in an hour to begin the breakfast without me."

Rebecca had hoped now that the marriage had taken place that she could enjoy the fruits of her efforts for the rest of the evening in relative peace. But family always came first. She squared her shoulders and walked briskly toward the meeting. The timing of Peter's arrival could not have been worse.

Peter Warner stood in the center of the room and smiled when she approached. He had always been a thin, ambitious man, and since inheriting her late home and the entirety of her husband's estate, barring her jointure, he had not changed one bit. He had argued about her marriage settlement, claiming a duke's daughter hardly required an income of her own. He had assumed she would return to live with her own family. Peter reminded her of her late husband far too much.

"Mr. Warner."

"Mrs. Warner."

She curtsied, and he offered a brief nod instead of bowing. Rebecca overlooked the insult implicit in his actions and begged him to sit. "What brings you to Stapleton, sir?"

"I should ask you the same?" he said as he took a place beside her. "Last I heard, you were gadding about London."

"My time was better spent than that. My sister made her presentation at court, and I was there to support her." But she had to wonder when Peter Warner had ever cared about what she did. After her husband's shocking infidelity had become widely known, he'd been the first to place the blame squarely on her shoulders. "I always come home at this time of year. I've been here for weeks now."

Peter Warner blinked. "Is that so?"

"Yes, always." She drew closer to him. "Is something the matter?"

"No. Perhaps it is nothing. I am on my way to London, so I thought I should drop by and see if you were here."

"That is kind of you to call, but unfortunately you've arrived on a momentous day."

Peter leaned closer as his voice dropped to a whisper. "Is the duke hosting another of his little parties?"

She nodded. She didn't like it when Peter got too close, or any man bar Rafferty, now. She had too much history with Peter to believe he was talking to her as a brother or even a friend. "There was a wedding today."

He looked at her sharply. "Whose?"

"My youngest sister has married our neighbor, Mr. Whitfield, and they were just made man and wife as you arrived. It will not be long before the wedding breakfast is to begin."

"I suppose you had a hand in making the match," he suggested, sitting down as if he planned to stay a while. "You were always so keen to pair people together, weren't you?"

Rebecca sat reluctantly. She had tried to match Peter with a good woman once, but he had not been interested in what she'd had to say. She'd heard he'd married since her husband had passed, but she'd not met the woman. "Not at all. My sister and Mr. Whitfield realized their mutual admiration had become love and matched themselves, really."

"Love?" Peter scoffed at the idea. "Or is it the meeting of two great fortunes."

"Money had had nothing to do with Jessica's choice of husband. How is everyone at home?"

He looked displeased by her question but shrugged. "Quite well. We manage very well without your interference."

She refused to let that remark upset her. She'd been happier without her husband's family in her life too. "I'm glad."

Warner talked then of the estate crops thriving, the home farm a storm had wreaked havoc across, fields of barley harvested months ago, and a dozen small things that mattered little to Rebecca now. Once upon a time, she would have cared a great deal. She would have worked day and night to make sure everything ran smoothly.

Not that her efforts had ever been appreciated. "You have had your hands full."

"Yes, indeed. It's been a profitable year so far."

She hoped he would leave soon. "And now you're at leisure to travel again. How marvelous."

Peter studied her. "Have you had any dealings lately with the solicitor. I assume you still have your business with Barclay."

"Yes, as a matter of fact I had a letter from him this week," she enthused. "He's in excellent health."

"What was the nature of the letter?" he asked, sitting forward.

His sudden question caught her off guard momentarily. Rebecca was not comfortable discussing anything about her finances, least of all with Peter.

"Nothing of importance," she said cautiously. Although they shared the same solicitor in London, what happened in her life was none of Peter's business. "He sent the usual quarterly report. I imagine you might have received yours recently too."

"I did and I will be questioning him about the contents when I see him."

Rebecca gulped. "Is there a problem?"

"Possibly." Peter frowned. "It may be nothing but I think it would be in our best interests to keep a closer watch on Barclay and how he manages our finances. There have been too many mistakes for my liking."

Rebecca gaped. "You too?"

Peter nodded but then suddenly stood up. "I should take my leave of you so you can get to the party."

Rebecca stood, too, feeling nothing but relief he was taking himself away. "Thank you for coming to warn me, Mr. Warner."

He studied her again. "I was only doing my duty. My brother would have wanted me to look out for you in this. Good day, madam."

A servant was waiting just beyond the threshold and showed him the way to the front door.

Once he was gone, Rebecca sank into a chair and put her head in her hand. Peter would never seek her out if he had any doubts about his suspicions. She would be wise to listen to him and return to London as soon as possible. She could leave at dawn tomorrow.

Chapter Thirteen

———◆———

Adam slapped Whitfield on the shoulder while he surveyed the flock of guests spilling out across the lawn. It was a merry group indeed, but he couldn't see Rebecca anywhere, and he was starting to wonder what had waylaid her. "How are you holding up, my friend?"

"Better than I imagined," Whitfield admitted quietly.

"Good. Good. I think your induction to the Westfall family is going very well," he joked.

Whitfield arched one brow. "Is that what this is?"

"I'm told one of the first rules of being a member of the Westfall family is to never faint," Adam admitted.

"You'd fail then. I heard all about your little spell after the carriage accident from Stapleton himself."

Of course, Stapleton had shared everything with Whitfield. They hardly kept secrets from each other. "The second rule is never to discuss any lapses of the first rule."

Whitfield laughed. "Is that written down anywhere?"

"I'm sure it must be. Becca will know."

"Becca, is it?" Whitfield turned, and his expression hinted at a grin. "That's not the first time you've spoken her name like that. I thought only the family dared."

"I like to live dangerously." Adam shrugged. "Rebecca simply does not suit her."

"And Becca does? I doubt she'd agree with you."

Adam smiled. "She never does. Where is she, by the way? I hope the intoxication of calling you brother for the first time didn't cause her to swoon and fail the first rule of being a Westfall."

Whitfield shook his head, laughing again. "I'm not at fault. I heard her brother-in-law has come—without warning or invitation, I might add. She's with him now."

"I hope it is nothing serious."

"I wouldn't know or dare ask her. But I know Rebecca's not on the best of terms with them, so I hope he goes away soon. Jessica is not happy about the delay. Her grace has held back the start of the wedding breakfast on account of Rebecca's absence."

Adam cursed under his breath. Damn the Warner family. They were keeping Rebecca from having any fun. That was not right. "That reminds me, I'd better go fetch my daughter before she thinks I've forgotten her. Excuse me."

Adam left the guests, but instead of fetching Ava straight away, he prowled the manor instead, dodging servants who were rushing to set up the rooms for dining.

He found Rebecca sitting alone with her head in her hands.

It looked like Mr. Warner had already gone. Concerned, he stepped into the room and closed the doors behind him.

Rebecca must have heard him because she lifted her head. Her smile was tentative. "What are you doing here?"

"I was on my way up to fetch Ava and saw you sitting here alone, so…"

Her brow rose. "Ava is upstairs, at the other end of the house, Rafferty."

He winked, and then swooped down to kiss her pretty lips in the hope of seeing her smile again. "The duchess is holding the wedding breakfast until you are free to join us."

"Oh, I asked her not to do that," Rebecca complained.

"Of course you did. But we wait for your

company regardless." He caressed her cheek. "What did Peter Warner want with you that makes you look so sad?"

She drew back, frowning. "I'm not sad."

And still, she shut him out. "I'd never tell anyone what you said to me in confidence. I'd take your secrets to the grave."

She smiled quickly. "There really is no great secret to share. Peter is on his way to London and came to say hello. He said he felt it was his duty to call on his brother's widow. He spent barely twenty minutes with me, and then he decided to continue on his way."

"Perhaps he did not want to delay your return to the party?"

"I'm sure that was it." She stood, hands spread wide. "I really don't mind such a brief interruption."

"You're not close then?"

"We haven't spoken in nearly two years. I haven't even met Peter's wife."

Men did not visit women they did not like—not unless they wanted something from them. Adam was perplexed by her account of the visit. "He sounds like an odd fellow," Adam said eventually, and then held out his arm. "The party awaits you, madam."

"Yes, true." She looked at his arm and shook her head. "It was kind of you to worry about my whereabouts but shouldn't you collect your daughter now?"

"Ah, yes. Ava will never forgive me if I forget her."

"I wouldn't forgive you, either," she warned.

Adam laughed and stole one more kiss. "I shall go and fetch my daughter as my lady commands then. See you soon."

Adam rushed upstairs to the nursery, where Ava would no doubt be looking out for him.

Instead, he found her standing in the center of the large room, clutching a handful of papers and with her arm outstretched. "Turn now," she cried, and the children hurried to do her bidding—some with disastrous consequences.

Some of the children were very young and very uncoordinated. Soon they were laughing so much, most toppled over. Ava stood in the center of it all, hands now planted on her hips. She ordered them all to get back up and try again.

Bemused by his daughter's behavior, Adam watched in silence for several minutes. Ava had clearly found her feet on this visit. The twins had her surrounded but they did not seem at all dangerous to her. He was glad because she might be seeing more of the pair very soon if he had his way.

He almost hated to take her away to the wedding breakfast, but he'd made a promise. "Ava," he called softly.

"Oh, you've come at last," Ava cried. She handed her papers to a nearby maid and then rushed to his side. "Where is Mrs. Warner?"

"Waiting downstairs for us both," he promised.

Ava waved to the children left behind and pulled him along toward the staircase.

"What were you doing back there?"

"Teaching everyone to dance. Mrs. Warner has been giving us lessons each day but she couldn't today because of the wedding."

He laughed. "Mrs. Warner gave you a chore?"

"I asked for something for us to do."

Adam chuckled. If, or rather when, he married Rebecca, Ava would definitely pick up more and more of her managing habits.

He brought Ava to her chair and sat down beside her just as the first course was served. Unfortunately, Rebecca had seated herself far from him and Ava. His daughter waved to her, and so did Adam without really thinking about it.

Rebecca blushed bright red and waved back with a very small hand gesture.

The food was spectacular, the array of dishes served sublime. If this was what being managed by Rebecca could be like, Adam was keen to secure such a future. He laughed through the speeches, mostly because Whitfield seemed extremely uncomfortable.

When the newly married couple finally slipped away from the guests hours later, Adam discovered he was envious. Not of Whitfield marrying Lady Jessica but the fact that his friend had someone to love openly.

Adam shouldn't complain. He'd won the interest of the lady of his choice, but he was uncertain of what the future might bring. Rebecca could say no to his proposal when he made it. She had not exactly embraced the idea that they could continue after the house party.

After Ava had returned to the nursery, Adam kept an eye on Rebecca, but he'd not found another opportunity to catch her alone to discuss their future. And he wanted to have such a discussion with her. More than anything, he felt an urge to ensure their relationship continued well beyond the next few days of the house party.

He suddenly saw his chance when a female servant beckoned to Rebecca, and she moved into the hall. He followed via an indirect route but came to a standstill when he reached the hall. Adam didn't see her at first because she had walked farther on. But he heard her voice, issuing instructions to wake her early tomorrow.

Adam reached her just as she dismissed the maid. "I have never enjoyed an evening more, Mrs. Warner."

"I'm glad." She glanced around. "It feels like a weight has lifted from my shoulders."

"And now the burden of spoiling your sister will fall on poor Whitfield's shoulders."

"I'm confident he'll manage," she assured him. "And probably won't complain."

"New husbands rarely do," Adam promised.

"Yes, I remember that. Men save their petulant displays for later."

Adam caught her tone of disapproval and peered at her. "You did not enjoy being married, did you?"

"I never said that," she said quietly.

Adam was learning to read between the lines to hear what she did not say. He could understand—she'd been betrayed and humiliated. It might take some doing to earn her trust and agreement to marry. Adam was optimistic that he could prove himself worthy eventually.

"I liked it," he confessed. "It was comforting to know that at the end of the day, I would have someone to crawl into bed with."

"I prefer sleeping alone."

"All evidence to the contrary. You hog the covers, madam," he complained with a soft laugh. They did well together in bed. Outside of it required perhaps a little more time for her to become accustomed to the idea of him always being around. He nuzzled her neck. "I adore the scent on your skin. It is so unusual. What is it?

"Jasmine and coal tar," she whispered.

"Coal tar?"

"It is usually used for skin complaints but it works."

"Remarkable. I have both of those at Gable Park, but I never thought they would do so well together."

"Shh, it's a secret."

He chuckled. "Do you ever wish you were the mistress of a large estate?" he asked. "Don't your fingers itch to tell someone what to do and benefit from it?"

"I benefit from that already." When she smiled, his heart skipped a beat. If they continued to get along, he would make sure she always had reason to.

He stepped back, holding out one hand. "Come with me," he whispered, beckoning Rebecca to join him in the shadows of a nearby chamber.

Although a frown immediately marred her brow, she glanced over her shoulder and then, to his delight, followed after him.

As soon as they had privacy, he pulled her closer then spun her around. He placed his hands on her shoulders, noting her muscles were tight enough to play music upon with a bow. He kneaded her flesh a moment, earning what sounded like a very definite moan of gratitude, and then kissed her neck. She was lovely—when she wasn't angry with him. "You've accomplished so much. You must be pleased."

"I think my father is pleased."

Adam resumed nuzzling her neck, sliding his hands around her body possessively.

"I can't stay," she whispered.

"A minute more," he begged softly. "I thought this might make you feel good. You've been run off your feet for days chasing your family about. You need a little attention, too."

"You're very good at that, but…"

"You'll go back and stay on duty until the end of it all?" he finished for her.

"I had planned to. That's why I wasn't going to dance tonight."

"I wondered why you refused, but I still want you."

She raised her eyes slowly. "I can't see you tonight."

She looked so sad about it, Adam cupped her cheek and pressed a kiss to her brow. There would be plenty of time to be together if he had his way. "I understand. You can't bear to let any of them down, can you?"

She shook her head.

"Go back then. I'll still be yours tomorrow night," he promised with a grin. He wasn't leaving Stapleton until the duke kicked him out.

"Adam, there is something I must tell you before I go."

Adam quickly pressed a finger to her lips. "You don't have to say a word. I know you'll miss me tonight."

Although she nodded, another frown formed on her brow. "I have to go. Farewell."

"Until tomorrow." Adam allowed Rebecca to walk away. But tomorrow and the days that followed, he would formulate a plan to woo her for good.

He strolled back to the guests and met the Duke of Stapleton before he'd gone too far. The duke's smile was strained. "I need a drink."

Adam agreed to join him. He could drink now because he would not risk offending Rebecca's delicate sensibilities later that night. Adam followed the duke into his study and took whatever he was offered. "A toast to a wonderful marriage just begun," he cried.

The duke agreed absently and downed his drink.

Adam put his glass down. "Is something wrong?"

Stapleton nodded. "Not exactly but my wife has taken ill again, and I do not like feeling torn."

"Oh, I'm sorry to hear that. Her grace seemed

well an hour ago when I spoke to her last."

"The sickness comes and goes more often than I ever knew." The duke looked up at the ceiling. "I've just found out my wife has been hiding that fact from me for weeks now. If not for Rebecca's help, I now know the wedding might never have taken place today."

"Your daughter is a skilled hostess," Adam noted. But then he realized that if the duchess was still ailing, Rebecca would assume her duties again for what remained of the house party, and perhaps beyond that, too. He was disappointed Rebecca might have only a little time for him, and only at night.

"I had hoped to go to London." The duke rubbed his hand over his face and yawned.

"When?"

The duke pulled out his pocket watch. "In a few hours."

"That's sudden, but I'm sure your daughters will be only too happy to keep an eye on her grace."

"I'm sure they would, but I would be happier if Rebecca were staying," the duke muttered before turning away to refill a glass.

In doing so, Stapleton missed Adam's utter shock.

Adam eased to the front of his chair, anxious to hear more. "I never heard that she was leaving tomorrow," he began evenly enough, but he quickly experienced alarm that his lover had had enough of him.

"No one knows yet that she plans to slip away at dawn. Damn girl drives her poor father to drink," the duke complained as he downed another glass.

Adam stood and collected his own glass. He sipped slowly, but it didn't help him feel any better. "Why is she going to London?"

The duke exhaled. "A small inconvenience. Nothing for anyone to worry about."

But Adam was immediately concerned. First, her brother-in-law drops by unexpectedly, and Rebecca won't tell him why, and now she is rushing off to London. Something was definitely going on with her—and he would get to the bottom of it before he decided how to confront her, or if he even should. "I'm glad."

Adam finished his drink and, after a moment of consideration, he poured another for the duke, too, making sure the duke's glass was fuller than his own.

Adam drank slowly, biding his time until the duke was feeling the effects. Then he carefully posed the questions that would help him discover everything he needed to know about Rebecca's sudden London trip.

Chapter Fourteen

Lord Rafferty, at last, exited the carriage outside a busy coaching inn on the way to London and left Rebecca in the company of his daughter and her maid. They'd been traveling for hours from Stapleton now, and Rebecca longed to escape the close confines and the tense atmosphere—the result of being nearly abducted by the earl.

Apparently, sometime during last evening, Rafferty had learned of her journey to London and obtained her father's blessing to convey her there in his own carriage.

Rafferty had not intended to travel to London as of yesterday afternoon. He'd given every indication that he would remain at Stapleton Manor for many more days yet. Rebecca had hoped to complete her London errand and return to Stapleton—and to him, if he was still there waiting.

But now they were traveling together, and he had not questioned her once about her reason for the trip. That was unusual, because Rafferty had taken to questioning everything she did lately. Rebecca was concerned that her father had let something slip last night about her troubles, too. Why else might Rafferty have felt compelled to make a journey that so closely coincided with her own out of the blue?

Rebecca leaned forward and helped Ava return her slippers to her feet. The girl had slept for most of the day, thankfully, and never questioned where her father was taking her. "We must be careful here and stay together," she warned the girl. Nancy did not need to be told that coaching inns were dangerous places for women on their own. Ava would have her father's protection, of course, but Ava did not always do as she was told. She had escaped the Stapleton nursery several times on her own, and it was only good luck that Rebecca had come across her.

"I'll keep my eye on the girl," Nancy promised. "Tonight, too."

Rebecca appreciated it, but she worried about that and the other sly comments her maid had uttered along the journey to London. No matter that the earl had kept his head in a book while in the carriage, Nancy seemed to suspect that Rebecca was involved somehow with him. Her servant had glanced between them for the whole of the trip and began to smile as soon as Rafferty announced they would be stopping here overnight.

Rebecca peered out of the carriage at the dusty inn yard. She had never stopped at this particular coaching inn before and trusted that Rafferty had chosen well.

Rafferty returned then, looking a bit rumpled and weary, but he was smiling. He had a groom open the door again and put down the steps. He thrust out his hand to Rebecca. "The accommodations are arranged, madam. Let us go in."

Rebecca accepted Rafferty's help gladly but dropped his hand as soon as possible. Eager for a moment alone, she hurried into the building ahead of everyone and was greeted by the innkeeper.

"Lady Rafferty, welcome to our humble establishment," the man said.

Rebecca nearly choked on hearing the false title tumble from his lips. Lady Rafferty indeed? She forced a smile though.

The man smiled warmly. "Your husband insisted that tea be provided in the private dining room as soon as you've refreshed yourself from your journey."

"Thank you." Rebecca swept past him with

her most regal smile firmly in place but once alone, slapped her hand to her head. She could definitely feel a headache coming on. Rafferty seemed determined to make her life harder than it already was.

When she returned to the hallway after freshening up, she heard Rafferty laughing along with others. The taproom was in that direction, she thought, but she hoped he would join her soon so she could give him a piece of her mind—preferably before he was too drunk to hear how upset she was with him.

A maid directed her to a pleasant chamber far away from the taproom, and the blessed tea was already waiting on the long table. She sat, allowed the maid to serve her and sipped— biding her time until Rafferty joined her.

When Lady Ava and Lord Rafferty came in together, unfortunately, all she could do was scowl at him and continue to wait for her chance to speak to him alone.

Rafferty signaled the servant to fill two teacups and then dismissed them with a flick of his long fingers.

"I'm surprised you are not holding a tankard," she grumbled softly.

"People can change when they want to," he murmured, and then took a sip of his tea. "The few travelers in the taproom report the road ahead is in excellent condition."

She huffed at the news and looked his way.

Rafferty had changed in the past few weeks. She had to give him credit for that. But how long would such a miracle of his sobriety last or his choice of sedate waistcoats to wear continue?

She considered what to do. Only Ava was with them at the moment, and she had her face pressed to the windowpane, watching the yard below. Now might be the only chance she got for conversation before she retired for the night.

She caught Rafferty's eye to whisper, "Who do you think will believe this ruse you've concocted?"

"Everyone, unless you give yourself away by continuing to protest my decisions—designed, I might add, to protect your reputation," Rafferty said, sitting beside her. "Smile. No one knows us here, and Ava understands the necessity of a little harmless deception."

"So it will all work out—until we come face to face with someone we know," she snapped. "I told my father that I do not need an escort to London. Why are you going to London?"

"I have my reasons." Rafferty looked beyond Rebecca. "Ava, come away from the windows."

"But Papa, a fancy carriage just drove past."

The earl chuckled softly. "We arrived in just such a conveyance. Or is Papa's new carriage not good enough for you? Come back to the table now before I'm accused of rearing a heathen. Show her your prettiest manners."

The girl skipped to a chair, a look of chagrin on her face. But then she smiled. "Sorry, Mama," she said with an exaggerated wink.

Rebecca put her head in her hand. At least the girl seemed happy playing along with her father's ridiculous deception. She had no idea the trouble her father's ruse could land them in.

She lifted her head and squinted at the girl and then her father. Even though she liked Lady Ava, with her now sitting so close, Rebecca could not even whisper her complaints in Rafferty's ear without the girl hearing every word. He'd just maneuvered her into silence.

She fumed.

When the tea had been consumed in near silence, the innkeeper's wife returned with servants who rushed to place an array of dishes at the other end of the table. Nancy returned then, too, with assurances that the rooms the earl had rented for the night were prepared.

After they had eaten, she would send Lady Ava away to be with her maid and then she would exchange a few dozen private words with the earl. She was looking forward to that.

The earl smiled at her suddenly. "Let us eat. It has been a very long day, and I'm sure you ladies would like to retire for the night as soon as possible."

After she'd eaten, and had sliced Rafferty to ribbons, Rebecca intended to sleep alone.

They moved to the other end of the table, and although Nancy tried to serve, Rafferty sent her to her chair. He served Rebecca first and then his daughter, and the maid, too. There was wine on the table, but he poured only a little for himself and some for Rebecca. Ava and Nancy had milk.

Rebecca quickly discovered she wasn't very hungry after all. She moved the surprisingly good beef stew and potatoes around her plate endlessly and then pushed it away.

Rafferty noticed the half-eaten plate of food but said nothing about it beyond raising one brow in surprise. He continued eating, and entertained his daughter and Nancy with tales of his past travels. The girl lapped up the stories, hanging on her father's words in a sweet way that had Rebecca smiling.

Seeing them so happy together made Rebecca's irritation lessen. She did not know much about Rafferty's interests, but he certainly told a good story about his life. She'd never had reason to know him better until now, and almost against her will, she became fascinated by watching him talk. Perhaps he had a good excuse for being here after all.

Rafferty brushed at the crumbs on his lap at

the end of the meal. "Time for bed, my girl."

"But Papa—"

"No. No. We will be rising with the sun tomorrow to reach London in good time."

The girl came around and hugged her father tightly about the neck. Rebecca took the opportunity to gesture to Nancy to go with the girl. Nancy smirked at her then quickly wiped away the expression when Rebecca scowled.

Ava approached her with a look of uncertainty on her face. "Goodnight, Mama," she said softly.

Rebecca would not play along willingly. "Good night, Lady Ava. Pleasant dreams."

Ava suddenly embraced her before scurrying toward Nancy and slipping from the room.

She turned her attention on Rafferty as soon as the door shut. "What is the meaning of this trip of yours?"

"Can I not decide to travel to London at short notice?"

"No, you cannot. You intended to remain at Stapleton for the next few days."

"Plans change. I discovered I have pressing business to attend to in London."

"What business could you possibly have there that is so urgent? There were no messengers come to the estate yesterday for you, and you received no letters in the week before that."

His lips lifted into a smile. "Already managing me, Becca."

She scowled again. She had been keeping an eye on Rafferty's comings and goings but wouldn't admit to it now. She *had* engaged in intimate relations with the man. She would not have her happiness destroyed ever again because she had misjudged his character. "My name is Rebecca Warner. Mrs. Rebecca Warner."

He shrugged. "The name doesn't suit you."

"That is not your decision to make. Please address me properly once we leave this establishment. I will not be a party to continuing such a wild and ludicrous tale as you've concocted for our stay."

He sat forward suddenly, tapping his fingers on the table between them. "What if I told you the business that takes me to London is you?"

She felt her insides take a little swooping dive at his confession. "Me?"

"It came to my attention very late last night that you were leaving the estate—without saying goodbye, I might add."

"I tried to tell you…" She trailed off.

"You should have tried harder." He raked his fingers through his hair. "At first I thought it was because of me that you were going, too."

"No." She blushed. "My decision had nothing to do with our affair."

"Damn it, woman, you could drive a man back to the bottle. Do you think all I care about is sex?"

She felt her face heating. "You do talk about it a lot."

"I care about *you*." He scowled now. "What the devil is going on? Is it true you are in dun territory?"

Rebecca stilled. "Did Father tell you that?"

"Something along those lines. Don't blame him now. I got him blind drunk to discover what he knew."

She scowled. "That wasn't very nice."

"Stapleton never remembers what he says when he's been in his cups, so I doubt he will realize. And in his drunken state, he stopped worrying about his wife's delicate health, at least for a while. He was torn about letting you go alone to sort this out, so I led him to the idea of conscripting me to take you in my carriage. He's happily at home now looking after his wife. Now give me the real story. It's impossible to believe you of all women could have run out of money."

Oh he *was* devious! "How do you know that?"

"You spend money like a miser and count every penny twice before you go to bed at night."

"I do not!" She was offended by that

description. She drew herself up straight. "There is nothing wrong with being cautious."

"Which is why I know you've been poorly used. Once your father told me what little he knew, I made my own arrangements."

"I don't need help," she warned. She stood quickly and turned away, walking to the window to hide her frustration. "I never ask for help from anyone," she said.

Rafferty followed her to the window, stopping close behind her. "You don't need me, but you will have me."

She turned to look at him, frowning in annoyance, "You are presumptuous."

"Oh, I know that." He brushed his fingers across her cheek. "We have started something, you and I. I feel compelled to understand you. You refuse to accept help from your father, the rest of your family I assume don't have a clue. They are too wrapped up in their own busy lives to notice yours might be in jeopardy. You keep your secrets close to your chest but upon consideration, it's plain to see you were worried about this yesterday after Peter Warner had gone. But I'm not actually offering to solve your problems. I will, however, be by your side as you investigate whatever this is."

Something inside Rebecca softened so suddenly, she gasped out a sob.

"I'm here, Becca, and you are not alone

anymore," he whispered. "It will take more than a few harsh words and scowls between us to drive me away."

Although she had feared to trust any man, believing that she must stand on her own two feet, she was relieved by Rafferty's promise. Even in her marriage, she had felt alone.

Rafferty did not try to exert any control over her, really. He might follow along behind her though—large enough to intimidate anyone who might stand in her way. She reconsidered his coming with her. She could use Rafferty to her advantage *if* he kept his promise and stayed in the background until needed. "Thank you."

His arms wrapped around her and she fell against him, breathing deep. He was a kind man, the sort she once imagined her husband might be to her. She had liked lying in his arms at night, but this was even better.

His hands swept down her back in a soothing manner. "Tell me everything now."

So she did, and it felt good to unburden herself at last. She told him about Charlotte's habit of using Rebecca's connections to attend parties she otherwise would not be invited to. Convincing Rebecca to pay for a succession of small things they hadn't coin for at the time and never repaying her promptly or at all. The increased expense of her Bath holiday a year ago and the new invitation she'd just declined.

"Now it seems someone might be running up bills in my name again," she said. "My solicitor also manages my funds and he sends me a statement every quarter. But one of the expenses he included in the most recent was not mine."

He kissed the top of her head. "There's more. Go on."

Rebecca sighed. "Peter Warner really called to warn me he had uncovered similar discrepancies in his finances too," she whispered. "He has lost faith in Barclay and intends to confront him."

"As he should." He cupped head gently in one large hand, and she pressed her cheek into his palm. "Your father said your solicitor is next to useless."

"That is his opinion."

"Then tell me yours," he asked.

She blinked back tears at his question. "I have trusted Barclay since I became a widow. There have been a few minor mistakes but Peter's warning has me wondering if I've missed anything else. I feel it would be prudent to assess the situation myself so that is why I left without warning anyone but my father. Barclay has worked tirelessly for me over the years. I need to know I have not trusted the wrong man again."

"You are right to be cautious. A few quiet

words with him should give you the answers you seek."

Rebecca looked up quickly. "You're going to be a problem for me, aren't you?"

"Undoubtedly, yes," he promised with a grin. "I do not like it when my good friends are imposed upon."

Good friends? Was that how he thought of her? She didn't want that to be all they were to each other. "No violence."

"Trust me," he whispered before releasing her completely and stepping back.

She sighed. "That isn't easy for me."

"My dear woman, I've spent the last week in close proximity to you, getting in your way on purpose. I understand what you fear most of all now."

"What is that?"

"Depending on anyone for your happiness." He smiled quickly. "I promise you'll hardly notice I'm with you. If there is trouble, however, I happen to be on good terms with the London magistrate."

"I don't think a magistrate will be necessary for a series of minor mistakes made by a clerk in his employ."

"You should always plan for the worst while expecting the best," he said. "We'll visit Mr. Barclay together."

Rebecca worried her lip.

"What is it now?"

"What will people say if they notice you and I together?"

He moved to stand before her, his expression grave. "When will you understand that I'm not an enemy to your reputation? We will have your maid and my daughter tagging along as chaperones at all times."

She shook her head. "It would not be right to take Ava with us."

"The maid comes whether you want her to hear what is going on or not."

"She already knows," Rebecca admitted. "What do we do now?"

"Well, tonight, my lovely wife unfortunately must sleep alone because I told the innkeeper I snore quite terribly." He shrugged. "Beyond that, after your affairs are in order, I don't know."

Rebecca nodded slowly, but her mind was awhirl with uncertainty. Permanency had not been a consideration when she'd met with Rafferty the first time. Now, though…well it was indeed something that seemed very appealing.

Chapter Fifteen

Adam waited impatiently within the carriage as his card was presented at Rebecca's door the day after they'd arrived in London. They had parted company the afternoon before without making plans to see each other again. They had all been exhausted, but he did not think Rebecca had meant to forget him. Still, he had delivered himself at the time he deemed suitable for their outing—half afraid she'd gone on without him. There was no knocker on her door to announce her return to town. It was better that way too, in his opinion. The creditors would not come knocking.

A servant of the Upper Brook Street townhouse suddenly appeared at the door and pushed it wide. Rebecca appeared, and then she and her maid Nancy slipped down the stairs and into his carriage without delay. "Good morning."

"Good morning, Mrs. Warner. Nancy."

Rebecca's maid smiled quickly and took her place across the carriage while her mistress fidgeted at Adam's side.

He glanced her way. "The driver needs to know where to take us first."

Rebecca removed a paper from her reticule and read off a location for the waiting driver. "As quick as you can," she asked.

Adam chuckled. "The last time you said that, we destroyed a carriage and I had to have my head stitched. Please do not rush the journey, Mr. Chapman."

"Yes, my lord."

She smiled quickly. "How is Lady Ava this morning?"

"Surly. Ava misses you already." He looked out the window. Ava had not been happy to be left behind today. However, he had promised she could host a fine dinner to share with Rebecca soon. He carried an invitation in his pocket for that express purpose that he would deliver later when they were alone. "She begged to come see you."

Rebecca sighed. "I thought she understood."

"She has enjoyed your company a great deal. It is normal for her to become attached to the only friends she has made in her short life. How was your evening?"

Rebecca smiled. "I found last night a bit quiet. What did you do?"

"I had some errands to run and then went to the club. I ran into an old friend there. Sir John Culpepper will be only to happy to lend any assistance we might require."

The maid was following their exchange with unbridled curiosity so he said no more for now.

Thank heavens the solicitor's office was only a short distance away.

They stopped before an impressive building. Clearly the solicitor was doing well. Adam assisted Rebecca exit the carriage and waited till the maid joined them. He escorted Rebecca up the stairs and into the entrance hall. To one side, he heard voices engaged in a heated debate.

"This way," Rebecca said as she strode forward toward a tall side desk and rang a little brass bell. A neatly dressed young man suddenly appeared from the back, smiling broadly. "Welcome to Barclay & Jones. How may I help you?"

"I should like to speak with Mr. Barclay," Rebecca explained.

The fellow winced a little. "I am afraid that is quite impossible today, madam."

"Is he here?" Adam asked quickly before Rebecca could identify herself as a client. Adam thought an ambush might be the best way to obtain the reassurances she sought.

"Yes, of course, sir. But I am afraid he is in a meeting with a very important client."

Adam presented his card to the fellow. "The matter is of great importance to me."

The clerk's eyes grew round. "Please forgive me, my lord. I did not recognize you."

"Of course, I am not a client of this establishment. Not *yet*, anyway," he murmured. What is your name, sir?"

"It is Gibbons. Anthony Gibbons, my lord." He began flicking through an appointment book. "Mr. Barclay could see you in a few days."

"Today," Adam insisted.

"I'll see what I can do."

"Good." He intended to get Rebecca a meeting any way he could. "Do you have somewhere private we might wait for Mr. Barclay?"

The fellow bit his lip as he glanced toward the distant doorway where Adam had heard raised in argument before. All had grown quiet inside.

Gibbons seemed a smart fellow, proved it too when he quickly rounded the desk and gestured Adam toward another doorway further down the hall. "This way, if you please, my lord."

Adam smiled as he ushered Rebecca into

the offered room and held a seat for her before he looked around properly. The place was full of files and paperwork. It was a busy practice. He could see how mistakes might be made.

Adam made sure that Rebecca's maid had a chair and turned back to Gibbons. "There's nothing we need now but for Barclay to see us. You may return to your duties, sir."

"Very good, sir."

When the fellow had gone on his way, clearly reluctant to do so, Rebecca turned to Adam to whisper. "I've only met with Barclay in the library at the front before. This must be his private office."

"I thought it must be too."

Rebecca leaned toward him. "The clerk would have sent me away but for you."

"Possibly," he said. "That would have been a mistake."

They waited only ten minutes before a tall man with thinning hair burst into the room, full of apologies for keeping Adam waiting.

And then he noticed Rebecca perched at his side and his smile slipped away. "Mrs. Warner?"

"Mr. Barclay."

"I had no idea you'd be returning to Town."

"I arrived only yesterday."

The man glanced at Adam again but appeared very confused. Adam tipped his head toward Rebecca and then folded his arms across his chest. He was only there to intimidate so that Rebecca could conduct this interview.

Barclay turned his attention to Rebecca quickly. "How can I be of service, madam?"

"I have come to discuss the statement you sent to me last week."

"Unfortunately, the matter is still under investigation."

"What was there to investigate?" Adam cut in. "Clearly, Mrs. Warner was in Suffolk at the time the purchase was made."

Rebecca shushed him. "I was hoping you might allow me to view the paperwork."

"For what purpose? You say the bill was not yours to pay. I will deal with the matter and reprimanded the clerk involved if he has made a mistake."

If. Adam did not care for Mr. Barclay's tone at all.

"But you were sure it was mine in the beginning. Forgive me for being particular about this matter, but I simply cannot get the situation out of my mind. I have reviewed all my previous shopping expenditure twice already."

When the fellow hesitated, Adam uncrossed his arms and made sure it seemed he was about to interfere again. That seemed enough for Barclay to shuffle through the contents of his desk and obtain a much-handled brown folder. Adam noted the file was quite small.

As the file changed hands, he sat back.

Rebecca quickly acquainted herself with the contents of her file. He saw an accounting of numbers on several pages but also loose papers inserted at the back. Adam did not attempt to spy on her finances. He didn't need Rebecca to have a fortune in order to marry her. He waited patiently, watching Barclay instead.

Barclay smiled back until one page suddenly slipped out her file and fell to the floor.

Adam quickly returned it to her promptly and then looked at Barclay again. The fellow seemed unconcerned as Rebecca studied the returned page and when she reinserted it at the very end of the file without comment he smiled warmly at Rebecca. "I trust everything is in order."

"I understand the situation better now, sir." Rebecca handed the file back, but she was studying Barclay closely too. The same look that tended to unnerve lesser gentleman.

Barclay showed no sign of discomfort however and Adam relaxed.

"I am sorry that you've come for nothing, madam," Barclay said. "If you had but waited I would have had an answer for you before the end of the month."

Rebecca stood. "Thank you, Mr. Barclay,

for seeing me at such short notice. I look forward to reading your next quarterly report."

"Are you returning to Suffolk now?"

Adam glanced at Rebecca quickly, but she ignored him and bestowed a smile on the solicitor. "I am not sure, but I will write to tell you my travel plans as I usually do."

They had not talked about the future but Adam would any day now.

Adam nodded. "Good day Mr. Barclay."

"Lord Rafferty, I hope to see you again soon."

"Perhaps," he said without committing himself to another meeting. He escorted Rebecca out, noting that the door to the library were open but was no longer occupied.

He heard Rebecca ask to be taken to a new address.

"Mr. Garrick's Emporium of Fine Wares? Sounds impressive."

"I highly doubt it will be," she warned him.

"Not to worry. You'll have me for protection. I'm glad you asked me to escort you," Adam teased.

He noticed the maid grinning at his remark, but then turned back to the view as they left the part of London he knew best. "Who do you think was in library?"

"It was Peter Warner," Rebecca confessed. "I would recognize his voice anywhere."

"He wasn't happy."

"No he certainly was not." Rebecca leaned closer. "Whenever I meet with Barclay he carries my file to the library and back again. When he returned to his office after meeting with Peter he had nothing in his hands."

"Do you think he has taken his business elsewhere?"

"Possibly." Her brow furrowed. "Peter cannot tolerate incompetence and he was already suspicious when we last spoke."

"We are close, my lord," Mr. Chapman called.

The carriage came to a complete stop, and Adam looked out and immediately wished he was with any other woman. He didn't like the look of the neighborhood. "I don't suppose you would wait here and allow me to deal with this matter for you?"

Rebecca shook her head, smiling. "Try to remember your promise to me."

The warmth of her indulgent smile captivated Adam. Rebecca may not openly encourage him, but she charmed without even trying. He longed to pull her against him and kiss that mouth into temporary submission. "What are we doing here?"

She frowned. "The page that fell from my ledger was a bill for purchases in my name."

"How recent?"

"The very day I followed my family to Suffolk. I left very early that day so the purchases could not be mine."

"You arrived at Stapleton Manor earlier than usual."

"Exactly. I wrote to tell Barclay I had left, after I reached my father's estate. A woman could not be in two places at once unless there was some sort of pretense involved," she noted.

Adam studied the shop façade through narrowed eyes, not liking the implications. "Please allow me to go in first and get a look at the place. Give me a few minutes before you both follow. Pretend we do not know each other at first so I can gauge the shopkeeper's reaction to your identity."

"Very well."

Adam exited the carriage. As he'd ordered earlier, the carriage had stopped some distance from the business. Adam ambled down the footpath to Mr. Garrick's Emporium of Fine Wares. The outside did not impress him still, but he went in and looked around. He found himself in a tidy little shop that belied the mean exterior.

A rotund man wearing wire spectacles stood behind the counter and beamed. "Welcome to the emporium, sir."

Adam nodded and then looked about some more. It seemed a place where a man could buy almost anything he needed to make a good impression. He moved to one side and inspected a selection of walking canes. These were good quality items and reasonably priced, too.

But before he could investigate further, a movement at the window caught his eye. Rebecca had arrived—almost too soon.

She marched straight to the counter and the shopkeeper. "Good morning. Mr. Garrick, I assume?"

"Indeed I am." The fellow beamed.

"I believe you have billed me for purchases recently. My name is Mrs. Rebecca Warner, and I assure you we have never met before."

Garrick squinted at her, and Rebecca looked back at him in the most unfriendly fashion possible.

"You are not Mrs. Rebecca Warner," the shopkeeper corrected.

"I am the one you billed. My card.

The fellow squinted at the writing on the card, and then Adam noticed he tested the quality of the paper with his thumb. A frown appeared between his eyes but then it cleared, and he returned the card to her. "How can I help you today?"

"As you can see, my residence is on Upper Brook Street. It is the address to which you supposedly sent a gentleman's pocket watch.

Do you expect me to pay for an item that was not delivered?" she demanded impatiently.

Adam winced at her tone. Rebecca had every right to be angry but her temper would interfere with the inquiry.

Adam strolled to the counter and stopped when he reached Rebecca's side. "Is there a problem?"

Garrick glanced between them. "Who are you?"

Adam presented his card too. "Adam Croft, sixth Earl of Rafferty. Perhaps you could help the lady with her inquiry?"

The poor man fairly trembled. "Perhaps."

"Well, the lady and I are good friends." He gestured to Rebecca. "This is the honorable Mrs. Rebecca Warner, daughter of the Duke of Stapleton. We have come to ensure that you never bill her again for purchases she does not make."

Garrick squeaked and rushed around the counter. Thinking the man meant to escape, Adam hurried to block his path. But Garrick only reached the latch and locked them inside together. He turned slowly, face pale. "There must be some mistake."

"No mistake. I was not even in London on the day that pocket watch was purchased."

Garrick glanced at Adam and then back at Rebecca. "I don't want any trouble?"

"There will be none if you answer my questions honestly," Rebecca told him.

"Anything." He scurried around the shop and found two chairs. He offered Rebecca one and then one to Adam. Adam declined, and gestured for the older man to sit down instead. "Anything at all."

"The pocket watch. Do you remember who gave you my name?"

"A woman."

"Can you describe her?"

Garrick did. "I had no reason to believe she was lying," he told her. "She presented her card and seemed quite genuine."

"Do you still have it?"

"I'm sorry. The lady took it back I think."

Adam caught Rebecca's eye. "Any shopkeeper might believe she was you if they dressed the part and the shopkeeper did not to dig too deeply."

"That does not make me feel any better, Rafferty," she grumbled.

Adam set his hand on her shoulder to soothe her as he addressed the shopkeeper again. "What else do you remember about her? Anything at all is important."

"Not much really. The woman was elegantly dressed. Softly spoken. I've seen them come and go from a neighboring establishment many times now I think about it."

"Them?"

"Yes, she said she was to be married." The fellow suddenly grinned. "Would it be better if you could meet them?"

"You can arrange that? You know where they really live?"

The fellow shook his head. "No, I do not have their proper address, unfortunately, but on her last visit to my shop, the lady asked me if I could procure a special item I do not usually carry. A little something to sweeten her husband's mood, she said. It is for the anniversary of their first meeting I believe. I promised her I could and would have the item tomorrow. I expect her before I close at noon."

Adam grinned. "That is very good news. We can lie in wait and hopefully identify the woman and then we will follow her back to her own home to meet her husband."

Rebecca leaned forward. "What is it you were to procure for her?"

"A snuffbox."

Rebecca visibly flinched.

"Is that important?"

Rebecca said no, but Adam was not convinced it wasn't. A frown had formed on Rebecca's face again and she asked to go home.

Adam said their goodbyes and herded Rebecca and the silent maid back to the safety of the carriage. But he watched Rebecca closely the whole way back to Upper Brook Street. When they arrived at her townhouse, Adam was truly worried. "I'll escort you inside," he murmured.

Rebecca did not even try to stop him.

Adam handed her out, and she rushed up the stairs ahead of her maid. Once inside Rebecca dismissed her maid and turned to a nearby parlor.

Adam followed Rebecca inside.

"Could you close the door please," she asked. "I'll be with you in a moment."

Adam did and turned back to find Rebecca flipping through the pages of a small book.

"What are you looking for?"

She held up one hand, continuing to run her finger down each page. "There."

"What?"

She lifted her eyes to his. "I must be the worst judge of character of anyone that has ever lived."

He shook his head in denial. "That is simply not true."

Rebecca crossed the room and dropped into the seat next to him. "I always seem to place my faith in the wrong people only to be burned later."

"You are a kind woman," Adam promised. "If there is any fault in you is that you give too much of yourself."

"Or they try to take what is mine."

Adam slipped his arm around her back. "You know who visited that shop, don't you?"

Rebecca nodded, and then her face twisted with unbearable pain. She uttered a little wail and threw herself into Adam's arms. She sobbed, quite bitterly for a good long while as Adam tried his best to comfort her. After a while, he picked her up and sat her on his lap. With Rebecca secure in his arms, Adam let her cry as hard as she liked against his coat and then brought out his handkerchief. He pushed it under her nose. "Here, take this."

She took it from him but turned her face into his shoulder rather than looking at him.

"Did you know that the first rule of my family is that a good cry is allowed, nay even encouraged. Sob away."

She spluttered. "You're trying to make me feel better?"

"Is it working?"

"Yes it is." She sat up on his knees, dabbing at her tear stained face. "You're a better man than I gave you credit for. I was so cold to you for so long. How did you stand me?"

He took the handkerchief and soaked up her tears with it. "I'm an acquired taste. So are you. You're a good influence on me. Will you tell me now whom you suspect? I swear, I'll draw his cork if you want me to."

"No violence will be required from you, Adam," she warned.

Adam grinned because Rebecca had used his given name at last. Now they were really getting somewhere. "Tell me? No more stalling."

She tilted her head to the side and her expression grew pensive. "I might need your help proving the matter."

"That's what I'm here for. To help you."

"I might also need your help finding a new solicitor soon too."

Adam cursed at length.

"Language, Adam," Rebecca chided when he finished venting, but she was smiling at him fondly. "You are in the presence of a lady."

"Damn right I am." He kissed Rebecca soundly and they quickly made plans for the next day.

Chapter Sixteen

---◆---

"This is cozy," Adam whispered, nuzzling Rebecca's neck.

Rebecca was standing in his arms in the storeroom of Garrick's Emporium of Fine Wares the next day. They had been hiding here an hour, and her feet were already starting to ache. That was the only reason she'd allowed Adam to embrace her.

He seemed very good at holding her up. "What if they don't come?"

"Then we'll catch him tomorrow. Garrick won't complain."

"Of course not. Not with you spending your money in his shop."

"I'm planning for the future. When Ava is older, I'll need those walking canes to drive off her would be suitors. When this is over, you should buy something from the shop too.

There is a pretty lady's cane over there I've been admiring this past hour. I think it would suit you very well."

"Ridiculous. A frown is as good a deterrent as any and I certainly don't need a cane."

"Scowling works for you, not me. I like to be more hands-on with my conversations." His big hands rose and cupped her breasts.

To her mortification, Rebecca's nipples hardened under his palms. She had missed his touch these past few days but now was not the time for lovemaking. "Adam, not now."

"But why? You were just starting to enjoy it," he kissed her cheek but lowered his hands obediently. "When?"

She'd sent him home last night unsatisfied to be with his daughter. But tonight might be another matter. She had needs too, and he was very good at paying attention to those. "That depends?"

The shop door bell tinkled, and they both peered through the crack in the door. A woman entered the establishment, but she had blonde hair and walked unevenly. It wasn't her.

Rebecca leaned back against Adam and sighed. "She's not coming."

"Patience, Becca" he urged. "People will do almost anything for money when they care only for themselves," Rafferty warned just as the bell tinkled again and the blonde woman left.

When the bell rang again, Rebecca put her eye to the gap and saw a pretty India muslin on a woman entering the shop. When Rebecca saw the woman's face, her breath caught because she knew her very well indeed. She had hoped to be wrong about this.

Rafferty's grip tightened on her waist. "Wait. Is that who I think it is?"

"Indeed it is," Rebecca agreed quietly. Charlotte Benning. A woman Rebecca had considered a good friend until recent times. Charlotte had met Barclay a year ago today in his offices.

"Don't let her see you yet," Adam warned drawing Rebecca back a little more from the gap in the door.

But she saw Charlotte approach the shopkeeper, smiling warmly. "Has my order come in?"

The bell chimed again and a gentleman of means entered the shop.

"That's Sir John," Adam whispered. "I'll introduce him to you later."

"Your order? Oh, forgive me," Mr. Garrick begged. "My memory is atrocious today. Could you remind me what your name is again?"

The woman beamed. "It is Mrs. Rebecca Warner of Upper Brook Street."

The magistrate, in the act of inspecting walking canes, clearly heard the woman because he turned to look at Charlotte frowning.

"Ah, yes. The snuffbox," Garrick said aloud. "I have it right here. Just a moment."

Rebecca was so devastated she turned away. She'd know Charlotte had no qualms in asking for trinkets when they were shopping. She'd never imagined she'd try to impersonate her.

"Oh, it is just what I hoped for," Charlotte exclaimed as she examined the tiny box. "Do send the bill to my solicitor for settlement as usual."

Rebecca was distraught. Charlotte clearly knew what she was doing.

"Not yet," Adam whispered holding her back as the door chimes rang out again.

Rebecca froze. It was her solicitor, Mr. Barclay.

Barclay strode straight to Charlotte's side. "My dear, what are you doing in this shop again," he demanded. "The carriage is waiting to take us home."

Charlotte turned, smiling. "Oh no, you'll spoil my surprise, my love."

"My love?" Adam asked quietly. "Are they in this together?"

Rebecca squinted at the pair and couldn't miss the look of love on their faces. "It seems so."

Charlotte darted back to the counter and collected her ill-gotten gains as other customers entered the shop. She took her present to Barclay, the snuffbox sitting proudly on the palm of her hand. "For you. To celebrate the anniversary of meeting each other."

Barclay's eyes twinkled. "You shouldn't have spent your pin money on me."

"I didn't," she said with a sly wink to him. "It is a gift from the woman who brought us together."

Barclay sighed and Rebecca seethed.

She was betrayed yet again by people she trusted. She had considered Barclay an upstanding gentleman but clearly marriage had changed him and not for the better.

Sir John jerked his head toward the couple urgently.

Rebecca closed her eyes briefly and then pushed open the door, aware that Adam followed close behind. She stepped out into the shop and glared.

Mr. Barclay was paid well enough not to need to steal from his clients. She was furious and did not bother to hide her feelings from anyone in the establishment.

Barclay paled when he noticed Rebecca and made a grab for Charlotte's hand. He started to pull the woman toward the door, but the magistrate's men were there to block his path.

Rebecca approached the pair and shook her head. "What did I ever do to either of you to treat me so poorly? I introduced you."

Charlotte was the first to recover her composure. "Becca, dear. It is not what you think."

"I heard you assume my identity to buy this man, your husband I presume, a pretty trinket to add to his collection of ugly snuffboxes."

Barclay colored. "I have never encouraged her."

"You never stopped her, though, did you?" She shook her head. "Shame on you both for stealing from me."

"But you have so much," Charlotte protested. "We were desperate to marry but without a fortune of my own I had no choice."

"By my calculation I had just enough to last my life time," Rebecca argued. "But there was never any room for extravagance."

The magistrate stepped between them and Rebecca was glad. Charlotte couldn't be allowed the chance to talk Rebecca out of having her prosecuted.

"You are both under arrest for the wrongful impersonation of the Duke of Stapleton's daughter, thievery by deception, knowingly misappropriating funds belonging to Mrs. Rebecca Warner, and others and for bringing the legal profession into disrepute," Sir John warned. "Take them into custody."

Barclay struggled but he was no match for

the men Sir John had brought with him. Charlotte went more quietly.

The shopkeeper joined Rebecca. "It is hard to pretend innocence when caught in the act." "Indeed." Rebecca hugged herself. "This will be hardest for Charlotte's family."

"Don't you dare feel sorry for anyone," Adam warned, putting his arm around her shoulders. "They deserve every embarrassment for the pain they've put you through."

"They do indeed," she said as she drew Rafferty even closer.

Rebecca sighed but looked to the grinning magistrate. "I heard Barclay say they've been shopping today. Would your men please try to find their carriage and question the driver about where their journey today has taken them? Those bills will need to be paid—but from the appropriate accounts this time."

"I had planned to do just that," Sir John said before bowing. "It will take time to assess the depths of their thievery but I will let you know the outcome. By all accounts so far, Barclay has been skimming from a number of accounts."

Adam cleared his throat. "I paid a call to Peter Warner after I left you last night and encouraged him to call upon Sir John as early as possible and share his concerns too."

"I'm grateful you did because he was not the only one." Sir John bowed to her. "It's been a pleasure, madam, and I hope to see much more of you soon. I'm not sure Rafferty deserves you though."

"Go away, man," Adam said as he gestured to the door. "You've more criminals to catch out there."

Rebecca watched the magistrate go. Mr. Garrick hurried back behind his counter as soon as they were gone. Rebecca turned in Adam's arms slowly. He'd kept his word and hadn't taken over. "Thank you," she whispered.

"Are you happy now?"

"I am content." Almost. There was one other concern she had but trusted that after today's events Adam would eventually bring the matter up.

"I'm glad." He collected his pair of canes from Mr. Garrick and tucked them under his arm. "Shall we go home?"

Home. But Rebecca's ideas of home had changed. She bid farewell to the shopkeeper and then tucked her arm through Adam's as they walked toward his waiting carriage. His grooms grinned upon their return. They'd known what was going on inside the shop and most had stood lookout with the magistrate's men. Adam tossed his new canes up to one and then helped Rebecca enter the carriage.

She sat back against the squabs and sighed in pleasure, glad to be alone with Adam at last.

"This is a very comfortable town carriage."

"I'm glad you like it," he said as he sat beside her.

The carriage got underway, and Rebecca leaned a little toward him. "I'm relieved its over."

"Very satisfying, madam," Adam agreed. "I never met the man before, but I did enjoy watching him squirm when you confronted him."

Rebecca shook her head sadly. "He wasn't even embarrassed that he'd been stealing from me. Do you think he took very much from his other clients?"

"Hard to say," Rafferty said. "Sir John will investigate as promised."

"I never imagined Charlotte would do such a thing."

"She was poor and saw a way to better her life," Rafferty murmured and turned. He brushed his fingers over her cheek gently smiling. "But no matter. You've another friend to play with now."

She glanced at Adam's face. "Only friends?"

"More than that," he promised. "In fact you have a family just waiting to be claimed. Tonight in fact if that is not too soon for you?"

She understood what he wasn't saying, but she had to check. "Did you arrange to get a special license to marry me?"

"I did indeed. Presumptuous, I know but I took a leaf out of your book and made a list—with only one item on it. I have a vicar waiting for word from me to marry us at a moments notice. Why we could be married in a few hours and then you could put your husband to bed too."

Rebecca laughed softly. "Is sex all you think about?"

"I think about you," he confessed and then looked down. "But it is hard not to think about intimacy when your fingers are gripping my thigh like that. Is there something more I can do for you today, madam?"

"A child, Adam," she whispered. "I want a family."

Rafferty kissed her fiercely and drew back to stare into her eyes. "A babe might take a little more time than a few hours to bring about, but in the meantime, I assure you Ava is desperately keen to call you Mother."

"I want to see her right now," she whispered.

Adam knocked on the roof urgently. "To the townhouse as quick as you can, Mr. Chapman. We're getting married."

The carriage immediately picked up speed. "Is that not a dangerous request to make when we are alone in a carriage?"

Adam captured her hand and pressed a kiss

to the back of it. "What matters is that we are together and soon will always be."

"And I you," she promised. "Whoever would have thought we might make a match of it?"

"No one at all." He laughed. "Will it not be the most delicious shock to your family when we return to Suffolk as a family?"

"When will that be?"

"Whenever you want to return to Stapleton I suppose," he promised with a wink. "I mean to be an accommodating husband. If you need to be at Stapleton, I'll not complain as long as I may join you there."

Rebecca's eyes misted with happiness at his announcement. It meant so much that he considered her need to be with her family. "And I will be a very good wife to you."

She slowly dragged her fingers down Adam's chest, noting with pleasure he'd taken to wearing muted colored waistcoats recently. She assumed he'd done it to please her sensibilities, and that gave her hope for the future. She lowered her hand further until he groaned.

"Yes, love. Tell me more," he whispered. "Show me."

A little impropriety wouldn't even matter if they were to marry tonight. She captured him and squeezed gently through his breeches as they made a hard turn that had them sliding sideways into each other. "I've got you this time," Rebecca promised.

"Be careful. Our future is in your hands," Adam warned, but he was grinning widely. "I love you for this and every other way you'll look after me, Becca."

"As you should, my lord," she whispered before kissing him soundly. She would have her hands full forever with him but she was looking forward to the challenge. Of course she would have to reorganize his entire household and take Ava under her wing as soon as possible.

If they fell out of love, and she really hoped they did not, she was consoled by the fact that she would have an earl of her own to annoy for the rest of her life.

If you enjoyed the story don't miss the rest of
the Saints and Sinners series…

The Duke and I

The Duke of Stapleton abhors Christmas nonsense,
but could a kiss exchanged under mistletoe with his
daughter's shy companion alter his opinion of the
season?

A Gentleman's Vow

To thwart an unwanted admirer, Lady Jessica
Westfall enlists the aid of Gideon Whitfield, her
dearest friend…and the love she's unknowingly
sought all along.

The Lady Tamed

A lady possessed of a fortune. A poor actor with a
shady past. It's the role of a lifetime…but their
contract said nothing about falling in love.

About Heather Boyd

——————◆——————

USA Today Bestselling Author Heather Boyd believes every character she creates deserves their own happily-ever-after—no matter how much trouble she puts them through. With that goal in mind, she writes steamy romances that skirt the boundaries of propriety to keep readers enthralled until the wee hours of the morning. Heather has published over 40 regency romance novels and shorter works full of daring seductions and distinguished rogues. She lives north of Sydney, Australia, with her trio of rogues and pair of four-legged overlords.

You can find details of her writing at
www.Heather-Boyd.com